Laura Reveal

P9-DFY-748

FLORENCE
FIASCO

By W. A. Sorrells

Illustrations by
Tom Bancroft and Rob Corley

Visit Karito Kids at karitokids.com.

The first books in the series of Karito Kids™ Adventures are dedicated to Steve and Jeff for their constant support and belief in KidsGive; Hannah and Will for their enthusiasm for KidsGive's goal of helping children around the world; Dave for his commitment and friendship; Andrea for her awesome work and dedication; Janet for her humor and belief in us; and last, but most certainly not least, Julie for her spirit and chutzpah. We couldn't have done it without you. Thank you for helping us imagine, create, and become.

—Love, Laura and Lisa

Your Code Number is 895572001070.

MORE THAN JUST A BOOK
Find Out All The Ways To Enjoy This Mystery Adventure

Each Karito Kids™ Adventure is much more than simply a book. By reading this book and visiting karitokids.com, you can explore countries, solve mysteries, and best of all help kids in need in other parts of the world. Get to know all the Karito Kids and become a part of an exciting new community of kids who care!

1. **Activate Your Charitable Donation**. If you purchased this book with a Karito Kids Doll, you may have already activated your donation. If you purchased this book by itself, go to karitokids.com and follow the online instructions to activate your donation. Three percent of the price of this book will be donated by KidsGive on your behalf to the children's charity Plan. The best part is that you will get to choose the cause to which you want your donation to go. You decide how you want to make a difference!

2. **Go to karitokids.com.** Check out our Karito Kids Book Blog where you can learn more about your favorite characters, where they live, and other fun stuff. You can even share what you think about each adventure, the actions they took, and the choices they made. You can find out what other kids think, too!

3. **Look For Culture Crossings**. While you're reading this story, keep your eyes open for places in the book where another country or culture is mentioned. Located within the story, illustrations, or journal, these places are called "Culture Crossings." When you locate a place in the book where another country (other than the country the story is about) is mentioned, go to karitokids.com and visit the "Culture Crossings" area and follow the online instructions. As with all Karito Kids games, you will also earn virtual *World Change* that can be accumulated and then donated by KidsGive on your behalf (as real money) to Plan. You might also find a few surprises!

4. **Solve Hidden Quests**. Each Karito Kid has so many adventures to share. Log onto karitokids.com and visit the "Hidden Quest" area to join her on additional quests. Just as with "Culture Crossings," you can earn virtual *World Change* that can be accumulated and donated by KidsGive on your behalf (as real money) to Plan.

Join up with other kids who are *Playing for World Change!*sm

WHAT IS KARITO KIDS™ ALL ABOUT?

We launched Karito Kids™ to help connect children around the world in a number of ways.

◎ The word "Karito" means charity and love of one's neighbor in the constructed language Esperanto. We hope that children around the world strengthen their connection with each other, creating a global village of peace and understanding.

◎ Each Karito Kids Doll helps children recognize and appreciate the beauty of the world's many different ethnicities.

◎ The book that accompanies each Karito Kid tells a fun story involving that girl. It brings to life another country and its culture and connects readers to the notion that children from across the world have many fundamental similarities.

◎ The unique online activation process will allow children to directly participate in giving. They can determine the cause to which they wish to direct a percentage of the purchase price of the product. They can receive updates on the project they choose and find out how they helped children somewhere else in the world.

◎ Combining traditional play with innovative interactive games provides your child a play date with kids all over the world. They will have the opportunity to write to children sponsored by KidsGive and learn how children live in other parts of the world.

◎ Our selected charity, Plan, is a non-profit organization that is bringing hope and help to more than 10 million children and their families in poor communities worldwide. KidsGive contributes 3% of the retail price to one charity to maximize the impact of change.

✿

uno

M y shoes! My shoes!"

Francesco del Sarto swept down the curved stairway in the lobby of our hotel, his shoulders wrapped in his trademark black cape.

"You!" Signore del Sarto pointed at my father. My father is the owner of the Pensione Russo, our family hotel in Florence, Italy. Signore Francesco del Sarto, the famous designer, was a guest at our hotel. "Where are my shoes? I demand to know!"

My father clasped his hands and pointed at Signore del Sarto's feet. "I believe, Signore, that your shoes are on your feet."

Signore del Sarto looked down at his feet, then looked at my father with a stunned look. "Not *these* shoes, you fool!" he shouted. "My new design. My diamond shoes. They were in my room only this morning. And now they're gone."

"No one has entered your room, Signore," Papa said. "No one except. . ." He hesitated, then looked toward me. "Well, my daughter, Gia, cleaned your room. But she's the only one."

"It was you then, little girl!" Signore del Sarto shouted. He pointed at me. "Give me back my diamond shoes!"

I stared at him. I had seen the shoes. How could I not have? They were the most beautiful shoes I had ever seen. I have to admit, I picked them up. I even put them on — which I know I never never should have done. It was completely against all the rules of the hotel. But if they hadn't been the most beautiful shoes in the world. . . .

"Tell me!" Signore del Sarto screamed. His face was red and his hands were trembling. "Tell me, you horrible, unspeakable little girl. Where are my shoes?"

I couldn't even speak. "I . . ." I swallowed. "Signore, I don't know."

"Liar!" He grabbed my father by the arm. "You get that little girl to give back my shoes, or I'll have her thrown in jail!"

"I'm sure there has been a mistake, signore," my father said, smiling pleasantly.

"I'll ruin you and your hotel! I'll have you all in jail!" He stormed back up the stairs, then paused at the landing, tossed his cape dramatically over his shoulder, and said, "Find my diamond shoes!"

due

TWO HOURS EARLIER

y family has owned Pensione Russo for seven generations. It's a very small hotel. There are only 19 rooms, plus a small restaurant on the ground floor. Once it was a *castello*—a sort of castle inside the city—owned by a noble family. It has a tower with slits in it for shooting arrows. It has suits of armor propped up here and there. It has old, murky paintings hanging on the walls. It's just about the coolest building you could imagine.

Except . . .

Except that the furniture is old and worn. Except that one room doesn't match the next. Except that the doors don't close properly. Except that it's hard to heat, hard to clean, and there isn't a thing in the building that works right. Not the toaster, not the hot water heater, not the televisions or the coffee makers.

"We do not have the most beautiful furniture," my father always says. "We do not have the

plushest carpets or satellite TV. But year after year, our guests return to us. Why?" Papa always clasps his fist in front of his chest at this point in the speech. "Because we have heart. The Pensione Russo has a soul. And all the satellite TV in the world will never give a hotel heart!"

He is so proud of our hotel. Not just proud. He *loves* the hotel. He loves every single thing about it. If he didn't have this hotel, I believe Papa would fall over dead the next day.

And me? Do *I* love the hotel?

Let's just say what I *really* love is designing clothes. Dresses, shoes, purses. I love buttons and straps and bows and gussets and seams and polka dots and plaids and silks and chiffons. I love beautiful things. I love music. I love parties. I love fashion and glamour and beauty and excitement.

But every day when I get up, I'm in a 19-room hotel where nothing works, where beds have to be made, floors swept, coffee brewed, breakfast served. Everyone in my family thinks making beds is the most important thing in the world.

Everyone except me!

So you can imagine how excited I was when I heard that Francesco del Sarto was coming to stay at the Pensione Russo. *The* Francesco del Sarto. The man who invented the wedge heel. The man who invented the micro-mini skirt. The del Sarto whose name is on one of the most famous stores in the world. The one whose name practically *means* glamour and excitement and beauty.

I was up in the room we rent to Signora Bernardi, the room in the tower with the arrow slits for windows. "So I can shoot at my enemies," as Signora Bernardi says.

"He's coming today!" I said to her.

"Who?" she asked, looking up from a book.

"Signore del Sarto."

Signora de Bernardi looked at me quizzically. "Del Sarto, del Sarto . . . ," she said vaguely.

"*Francesco* del Sarto!" I said, jumping up and down. "Who did you think I was talking about?"

Signora Bernardi smiled mischievously. "Ohhhhh!" she said. "*That* Signore del Sarto."

"I must admit," I said, "I'm a little surprised that he would stay at our hotel. This isn't exactly the Ritz."

"Ah, yes," Signora Bernardi said. "There's a story behind that."

"What do you mean?" I asked. I was always eager to hear gossip from the fashion world.

"Poor Francesco has fallen on hard times. I knew him, you know."

"You did?"

"Oh, yes," she said. "I used to model for him, back when we were both quite young." She looked off into the distance. "Of course, he went on to greatness after that."

"But why is he staying here?" I asked.

"Francesco is a genius," she said, "but he is a terrible businessman. At the height of his fame, he was swindled. The del Sarto line of clothes, the del Sarto stores in Milan and Paris and New York— he had to sell them all."

I frowned. "I don't understand. If his name is on it. . . ."

She shrugged. "A famous person's name is no different from Corn Flakes or Coca-Cola. It's a brand name. You can sell it, just like you'd sell a bar of soap. He was forced to sell his name and his businesses."

"But that's not fair. Who did it to him?"

Signora Bernardi scowled. "Giancarlo Bruno," she said. "That horrible little man."

"Giancarlo *Bruno*?" Giancarlo Bruno was the most famous designer in Italy. You've heard of him: Bruno shoes, Bruno bodywear, Bruno sport, Bruno intimates, Bruno everything.

"Francesco trained Giancarlo," Signora Bernardi said. "Eventually they became partners. And then one day —" Signora Bernardi snapped her fingers. "One day Francesco was out and Giancarlo owned everything." She shook her head sadly. "Poor Francesco, he simply disappeared. They say he hasn't designed anything in twenty years."

"That's so sad," I said.

"Fashion is a harsh mistress," Signora Bernardi said. "One day you're in. The next day you're out."

"Gia!" A voice came from the hallway. A loud, mean voice. My sister Cristina. My perfect sister who always makes beds perfectly and never forgets to empty the trash in a room. "Gia, get your lazy self out here!"

I sighed.

Signora Bernardi's eyes widened suddenly. "Fashion Week!" she said.

"What?"

"Last week it was Fashion Week in Milan. The introduction of all the big collections. This week it's here in Florence. All the Florentine designers are showing their spring lines."

"Gia! Hurry up!" It was Cristina again.

"It can mean only one thing," Signora Bernardi said. She clutched at her chest. "Francesco is going to show a new collection. He's making a comeback!"

"Giaaaaaaaaaa! The new guest is here."

"I've got to go, Signora," I said.

"Wait." Signora Bernardi reached out, adjusted my hair, and straightened my collar. "Perfect!" she said putting her finger under my chin and lifting it slightly. "Beauty in a woman begins with the neck. Always remember that."

"Giaaaaaaaaaaaaaaa!!"

"Agghh!" I said, laughing a little. Cristina is always so serious about her job at the hotel. Me? Not so much!

Signora Bernardi pointed to the door. "Go."

Francesco del Sarto was sweeping into the front door of the lobby just as I came down the stairs. He looked exactly like the photos I'd seen in the fashion magazines: tall, thin, with a small, pointed goatee and jet-black hair that fell to his shoulders. He was older than he was in the pictures, of course. Quite old, actually. Which made me think maybe the hair was dyed.

But his eyes were the same — piercing and black. He carried the same silver-headed cane that he'd carried in all the photos.

"Boy!" he shouted to my father. (As I was to learn, he never spoke at a normal volume. He was either shouting or talking so quietly that you almost couldn't hear him.) "Boy, take care of my baggage." He waved his cane at Cristina. "You! Prepare my room! I want the covers turned down precisely one meter. The windows must be open. A bottle of champagne, lightly chilled, must be placed on the bedside table. One can't think without fresh air and champagne."

He stopped, surveying the lobby with distaste. "You!" he said, pointing his cane at me. "You, do something about those wretched flowers. You'll need white peonies, white roses and . . . something blue!"

We had had the same silk flower arrangement sitting in the lobby since I was born. Now Signore del Sarto was asking us—no, *commanding* us—to change it. It was a little weird.

"This year, the entire world will be blue!" Signore del Sarto pronounced.

"Blue?" I said. Everything I had read in the magazines said yellow was going to be the big color this spring.

"I am del Sarto!" he said, fixing his piercing black eyes on me. "When del Sarto says everything will be blue, everything will be blue!"

He disappeared up the stairs. Signore del Sarto hadn't paused at the front desk to check in or even find out what room he was in.

I looked at Cristina. "Does he, uh, know where he's going or anything?"

She shook her head. "I don't think so."

We all stood there for a moment, feeling a little stunned and wondering what to do.

After a moment, Signore del Sarto appeared at the head of the stairs again. "What's wrong with you people?" He clapped his hands twice in rapid succession. "One of you silly creatures get up here and show me to my chambers!"

CHAPTER THREE

tre

YYYY NAAAAME IS KIMMMMMEL,"
The man said to my father. "WARREN
KIMMEL. FROM NEEEEWWWWWWWWWW
YOOOOORRRRRRRRRRRRRRRRRK. I HAVE A
RESSERRRRRRRVATION." Immediately after we
got Signore del Sarto settled into his room, more
guests arrived. Americans — a man, a woman, and
a girl about my age. The father wore a golf shirt
and khaki pants and loafers. The mother wore
huge gold bracelets, large, red-framed glasses and
high, teetery heels.

A lot of our American guests seem to think
that if you talk extremely loud and extremely
slowly, somebody will be able to understand them
even if that person doesn't speak English. I speak
some English, because in my school they teach it
starting when we're six years old.

As Papa was checking the man in, the girl
wandered around the lobby. She wore the most
beautiful clothes I had ever seen on a girl. They

must have cost hundreds and hundreds of euros. I was so envious! I could never afford clothes like that in a million years. Plus, I was wearing my boring old brown hotel uniform.

She noticed me looking at her and gave me a superior smile. "That's right, it's a genuine Giancarlo Bruno," she said as she ran her hand down the side of her dress. She wore sunglasses with the trademark "B" on the side. In rhinestones. Her shiny leather suitcase, her handbag, and her shoes all had the Bruno "B" on the side, too.

"I *totally* love Bruno!" she said. "But of course, you don't speak English. So you don't know what I'm saying." She gave me a big fake smile, like she was being really nice. Her teeth were perfect. "My name is Brittany Kimmel. How are you? You have pretty hair, but I must say, I'm not digging the brown dress. You look like an old lady in that." She kept smiling, thinking I didn't understand a word she was saying.

Well, yeah, I was thinking. *It's a hotel uniform! You think I would actually wear this if my parents didn't make me?*

But when you work at a hotel, sarcasm is not allowed. So I just pretended I didn't understand her. I just smiled right back. Papa says no matter what guests say, you just smile at them. But inside I felt really hurt.

"Brittany, now stop being difficult," the girl's dad said in a wheedling voice. "Come over here."

Brittany ignored him. "Daddy," she said walking around the lobby, "this is the yuckiest hotel I've ever seen. At least I'm getting my own room, aren't I?"

"Yes, you're getting your own room," the man said wearily. "This is the only hotel I could find. There's some big fashion show here this week and all the good hotels are booked."

"*Fashion show!*" Brittany said, eyes widening. "Can we go?"

"I suppose," her father said.

"Yay! Yay!" Brittany danced around, throwing her hands in the air. Then she said, "I'm gonna go explore this dump." She ran up the stairs.

I could smell her after she was gone. She was wearing some kind of strong perfume.

"Brittany, come back here," her father called.

"*Brit*'ny! *Brit*'ny! *Brit*'ny!" Her mother yelled, too. She had a loud, harsh voice, like a trumpet played by a kid.

The American girl paid them no attention whatsoever. Then she was gone.

I could see myself in the mirror on the far wall, a little dark-haired girl in a drab uniform and boring black shoes. That girl probably thought this is how I normally dress. If she could see me in my regular clothes, she'd see who I *really* was. Gia Russo, queen of fashion!

I just kept standing there staring at myself, thinking wistfully how nice it must be to be able to afford clothes like the American girl. I manage to dress pretty well, if I may say so myself, while spending practically nothing. Imagine what I could do with the money *she* had!

After the Americans had gone upstairs, the phone rang at the front desk. My father answered, then called to me. "Gia! Signore del Sarto needs something. Run up to his room and see what he needs, would you?"

Del Sarto was in our biggest room, the Grand Prince Suite. I knocked on the door nervously.

"Come in!" a voice called imperiously.

I timidly opened the door. Inside I found Signore del Sarto working furiously. He stood in the middle of the room in front of a dresser's dummy. He was adjusting a dress on it, using pins from a pincushion he wore on his wrist. The dress was made from three or four shades of pale blue silk taffeta. It had an Empire waist — that means a very high waistline, sometimes as high as right below the bust — with an unpleated skirt that hung all the way to the floor.

I couldn't move. It was the most gorgeous, wonderful thing I had ever seen.

Del Sarto finally glanced at me. "What are you gawking at, little girl?"

"It's so . . ." I couldn't even find the word.

"Yes, of course it is," he snapped. "I am del Sarto! Everything I create is *magnifico*." He glared at the dress. "But it's missing something."

I looked at it for a long time. Del Sarto seemed to have forgotten I was there. He stroked his face. He grimaced. He ran his hands through his long black hair. He groaned. He squinted.

I studied the dress, too. And suddenly I realized that he was right. As beautiful as it was, there was something missing. A little detail.

Something that would draw the whole design together and make it perfect.

"A bow," I said.

He looked at me sharply. "What?"

"A bow," I said. "Satin. Just one shade lighter." I walked up and put my finger where I thought the bow should go.

Del Sarto's jaw dropped. "A bow? A *bow!* Why, that is the silliest, most foolish idea I've ever heard. There is nothing in all of fashion more repulsive, more vulgar, than a bow!"

"But —"

"Del Sarto has spoken!" he shouted, slashing one hand through the air.

I saw a piece of ribbon lying on the bed. It was the perfect shade. I picked it up and formed it into a very small bow. A tiny bow, in fact. So small you almost couldn't see it. I just knew it was what the dress needed. I don't know why, but I *knew.*

"Anyway, what are you doing in my chambers, little girl?" del Sarto demanded.

"You called the front desk," I said, arranging the bow in my hand.

He looked at me suspiciously. "I did no such thing!"

"Yes, you did. You needed something."

"Impossible!"

I looked around the room. There were beautiful pale blue clothes everywhere: riding  pants with matching high glossy riding boots, skirts, evening gowns, shoes. They were scattered everywhere, as though he had dug through the trunks of clothes and thrown them into the air.

I couldn't help myself. I just started walking around the room, looking at everything. For me it was like being in a fairyland. I had always dreamed of seeing clothes like this. And now here they were. Handmade. Perfectly cut. Perfectly designed.

Some day, I thought. *Some day I will wear clothes like this!*

"What are you *doing?*" del Sarto shouted.

I didn't even realize it, but I had picked up a blue cashmere jacket and held it up in front of me. Del Sarto snatched it from my hands. "Get out! Get out, little girl! The idea of touching my creations!"

He pulled his hand back as if he was going to slap me across the face. I stared at him, frozen. I had had guests say nasty things before. But— *hitting* me?

Suddenly the designer froze, too. He actually looked a little taken aback at what he was about to do. "I'm sorry, little girl," he said softly, lowering his hand. "You must understand, these things are my whole life." He clutched the blue jacket to his chest. "For twenty years I have been like a dead man. I have been empty. But now I am making my comeback. This year I will show my first collection in twenty years. If it fails, then my life will be over."

Suddenly he just looked like a sad old man. A sad old man with pathetic dyed hair.

"If even a single one of my creations is damaged," he said, smoothing the blue cashmere, "the show will fail. And then. . ."

I felt a little sorry for him. But not *that* sorry. I mean, ten seconds ago he looked like he was going to slap me.

He stared sadly out the window. He seemed not to notice me at all. "I need more fabric," he muttered. "The collection is still not ready. I must go out and get more silk."

"It *does* need a bow," I said softly.

Then I ran out of the room. And slammed the door.

quattro

As I walked out into the hallway, I saw the American girl. She was standing next to the wall, running her hands down the dark wood paneling.

"Hey," she said to me in English. "Where's the secret passage? Huh? All these old buildings have secret passages."

I just looked at her.

"Oh, I forgot," she said. "You don't speak English."

I could smell her all the way down the hallway. Then I recognized it. She was wearing So Bruno!, the most expensive perfume Bruno made.

I smiled at her. "You smell like you took a bath in that stuff," I said in Italian. "It's tacky."

"Anyway," she said. "Who's that weird old man with the dyed hair? He looks like a creep."

From down the hall I could hear her mother yelling. "*Brit'ny! Brit'ny! Brit'ny! Come here! Brit'ny! Brit'ny! Brit'ny! Brit'ny! Brit'ny! Brit'ny! Brit'ny!*"

The American girl didn't even seem to notice. "I'm gonna find the secret passage and sneak into his room and see what he's doing," she said.

The door to Signore del Sarto's door burst open and del Sarto swept past us wearing his black cape.

"More silk," he muttered. "More silk. The collection just isn't ready."

Brittany snickered as Signore del Sarto disappeared down the hallway. "Bye," she said. "I'm gonna see what he's up to."

She tiptoed off after Signore del Sarto, a sneaky expression on her face.

I looked over at del Sarto's door. He was in such a hurry that he hadn't even closed it. In our hotel, all the rooms lock with an old-fashioned key. I walked over, inserted my hotel passkey and locked the room. If something were stolen from the room, del Sarto would probably go crazy. And that would be bad for the hotel.

Then something occurred to me. All those beautiful things. They were just sitting there inside the room. I looked up and down the hallway. Slowly, slowly I reached back into my pocket for the key. *What would be the harm?*

Suddenly my pulse was racing. Unless you

were cleaning, you never went into a guest's room. Never, ever. Not unless you were invited. Papa had said this to me a hundred times before.

But the thought of those dresses. Those blouses. Those shoes.

I slid the key slowly into the lock.

The next 10 minutes were like a dream. I picked up everything, held each beautiful item up to myself, looked at it in the mirror. The clothes were so beautiful. And they made me look like a whole new person. No one would ever say I was dressed like an old lady again—not if I were wearing these clothes.

I posed in the mirror, lifting my chin like Signora Bernardi told me to. Silks and cashmeres and cottons as soft as butter. I wanted to cry!

How could such a horrible man make such beautiful things? It didn't make sense.

Finally I had looked at almost everything. There was only one thing left, a pair of shoes. To my surprise, they fit me perfectly. They were low blue pumps. I stood in front of the mirror, held a skirt over my own dress, and looked down at the reflection of my feet. They didn't look like a little girl's feet. They looked like the feet of a princess.

I sighed, took off the shoes, and laid the skirt gently on the bed. Then I looked around the room.

At that point, the hotel owner's daughter in me took over. I thought about the requests Signore del Sarto had yelled as he came into the hotel. The bed was turned down exactly a meter, just like he'd asked. The window was open a crack to let in fresh air. Anything else?

Champagne. Hadn't he ordered champagne? There was no champagne in the room. I'd better remind Cristina. I wasn't allowed to deliver wine to the rooms.

I brushed a minuscule spot of dust off the desk, then walked out.

But then I stopped and just stood there. An urge had come over me that I couldn't stifle. Going in once was wrong. But to do what I was thinking about was not just wrong, it was stupid. I looked around to see if anybody was watching. At the far end of the hallway, I saw the little American

girl, peeping at me from around a corner. As soon as I spotted her, though, she pulled her head back around the corner and disappeared.

And then I couldn't help it. I was overcome by an urge so strong that I could do nothing to fight it. I went back inside the room, folded the tiny piece of blue ribbon into a bow, and held it up to the dress that hung on the dummy. It was perfect.

Truly, truly, truly perfect.

How many times in your life do you get to be part of something that's truly perfect? Not many, I'll tell you.

Without thinking, I pulled a pin from the dummy. My hand was shaking. Could I? Could I possibly?

Yes. I could.

I impaled the bow, pinning it to the dress.

And an hour later, Signore del Sarto was thundering down the stairs of the lobby, accusing me of stealing the shoes.

cinque

W hat are we going to do?" my mother was saying. "He said he would go to the police. I think he's serious."

The entire family was huddled in the kitchen, discussing the missing shoes.

"It would ruin our reputation!" Papa said.

"He seems a little absent-minded." Cristina said. "Do you suppose he might have just forgotten them?"

"No," I said.

Everybody turned and looked at me. I'm not just the baby of the family. I'm also the only person who doesn't really care about the reputation of the hotel. So my opinion is not taken seriously.

"We don't need your opinion," Cristina said. She was the spitting image of my father — with a thin face and plain features. Cristina is only two years older than I am. But she lives and breathes the hotel. So Mama and Papa take her seriously.

"I saw them," I said.

"How would you know which shoes he was talking about?" Cristina demanded.

"If somebody asked you how to set a table in the restaurant, would you know the right way to do it?"

"What does that have to do with anything?" Cristina asked impatiently.

"You know silverware," I said. "I know shoes."

Mama and Papa looked at each other. Mama shrugged. "She's right. Gia knows shoes."

"The shoes were here," I said. "Blue leather, with a diamond in the shape of a flower in the middle of each toe."

"I'm sure they were rhinestones," Cristina said.

I shook my head. "They were diamonds. Two karats each."

She squinted at me. "How do *you* know?"

I flushed. I couldn't tell them that I'd snuck into the room, that I'd picked them up and examined them minutely. That I'd actually *worn* them. "I just know," I said. And I did. I *knew*.

"Oh, well then!" Cristina rolled her eyes.

As we were talking, there was a loud knock on the door. Papa opened it and a small man with a very nice suit and a white handkerchief in

his breast pocket strolled into the room, looking around suspiciously. He had a puffy lower lip, like a very large rosebud, and one of the biggest noses I had ever seen.

"I am Vice Questore Ricci!" he said. "From the Polizia di Stato. I am here for the shoes."

The state police!

"Ah, Vice Questore," Papa said, "we are so glad you have arrived. We were just discussing the matter."

The police inspector ran one finger across the countertop, scrutinized it closely, then grimaced disdainfully. "Save the soft soap for your patrons, Signore. Let's not waste my time over a pair of shoes. Tell your little girl to give them back."

Everyone looked at me. "I don't *have* the shoes!" I said.

"If she says she doesn't have them, sir," Mama said, "then she doesn't have them."

"Signore del Sarto says you went into his room while he wasn't there," the police detective said to me.

I swallowed. He must have seen the bow I put on his dress. My eyes widened.

"Impossible!" my father said. "It is quite against the policy of the establishment. Unless she was cleaning the room or was invited in, she would never —" Papa turned to me. As he looked at me, he must have seen that my face had gone white. He frowned and cocked his head slightly. "Gia?"

I couldn't even speak.

"Gia!" Mama said. "Into a guest's room? You didn't!"

I started to cry. I felt all shivery inside.

"You see, I have done it again!" Vice Questore Ricci spread his arms wide. "I have solved the matter." He took the starched white handkerchief out of his breast pocket and handed it to me. "Blow your nose, young lady. Tell us where they are."

I wiped my eyes. "But I don't know!" I said.

The policeman glared down his long nose at me. "You admit you entered his room?"

I nodded.

"And did you tamper with his collection?"

"Uh —" I said. I felt sick to my stomach.

Mama held her hand to her mouth. Cristina stared at me, her thin, serious face going slightly pale. Papa's eyes narrowed.

"No!" Papa said. "You *touched* his things?"

"I just — I couldn't help myself. They were so beautiful!"

"Disgraceful!" The detective's voice rose. "Now tell me where the silly shoes are! If you don't, I shall be forced to arrest your father."

"My father?" I said. "But —"

"The shoes!" Vice Questore Ricci said, slapping his fist into his hand. "Now!"

I burst into tears again.

"Stop!" a voice said. "Stop that, you fool!"

35

We turned and saw Signore del Sarto standing in the doorway.

"If you want the truth from this child, then you need to understand what is in her little brain," Signore del Sarto said.

"Ah," Vice Questore Ricci said. "And you understand her brain?"

"I do. This child has a delicate and refined sensibility," he said. "Of *course* she couldn't help herself! The clothes are too beautiful to resist. Isn't that so, my child?"

I nodded, wondering where this was going.

Signore del Sarto entered the room slowly, his eyes fixed on mine. "You were caught up in the moment and you slipped them on."

I nodded again.

"You felt glorious. Like a princess. Yes?"

Another nod.

"And then, without another thought, you walked out of the room with the shoes still on your feet," the designer said.

I shook my head, my heart beating wildly. "No! I wanted to. But I didn't."

Signore del Sarto cocked his head and looked at me curiously. "I must have the shoes," he said.

"As long as the shoes are returned I will not be mad at you, my dear. For a moment I was angry. But now I am merely —" He cleared his throat and looked at me pleadingly. "Now I am merely desperate."

"But I *didn't* take them!" I said. "I just slipped my feet into them! But I took them off before I left the room. I know how much this show means to you. I wouldn't take that away from you!"

Signore del Sarto continued to study my face. "You know something," he said finally, turning to the police detective. "I believe her."

"I'm not sure I do," Vice Questore Ricci said.

Signore del Sarto pointed his silver-headed cane at Papa. "You, on the other hand, I hold responsible. This is *your* hotel. Those shoes are worth over 20,000 euros. If you do not find them, I shall expect repayment!" Then the designer spun with a whirl of his cape and disappeared from the room.

"I will get to the bottom of this!" Vice

Questore Ricci snatched his handkerchief back from me, folded it carefully, and inserted it into his breast pocket. "I warn you, Signore Russo, if I find that you are hiding something here, I will shut down your hotel! So I suggest you make every effort to find who took those shoes."

The police detective followed Signore del Sarto out the door.

Behind him, at the far end of the hall, I saw a figure creep out of the shadows and skulk down the hallway. It was Brittany, the American girl.

Then the door swung shut.

"Gia," my father said. "This is a very serious matter. I must ask you one last time, do you know where these shoes are?"

"I told you!" I said. "No!"

"You are in very, very big trouble," he said.

"I'm going to find those shoes," I said. "I promise."

"No, what you're going to do right now is go to your room."

"But —"

"To your room, Gia. Now."

"But —"

"The rest of us —" and he clapped his hands together. "We will begin to search!"

"But —"

Everyone else in the family walked out of the kitchen, leaving me alone.

"But I know who did it," I said miserably. "I know who stole the shoes."

sei

I went to my room and changed clothes immediately. I always feel better when I get out of my hotel uniform. And I was still smarting from what the American girl had said about me looking like an old lady.

Once I was finished dressing, I looked in the mirror and smiled. Much better! Don't you just feel better when you're dressed nicely? *I* do, that's for sure! The green dress showed off my hazel eyes and brought out the color in my cheeks.

While I was looking at myself, I realized that I couldn't just sit around in my dark old room. Not while the shoe thief was still out there!

I decided to find the shoes. I was almost sure I knew who had stolen them. That mean American girl was the only person who'd been in the hallway at the same time as me. She saw me go through the door. She was interested in Signore del Sarto. She was interested in fashion. And she even said she would try to find a way into his room.

It was obvious Brittany had taken the shoes. I just had to find out where she had put them.

I left my room and tiptoed into the kitchen, waited for about two minutes, then peeked out of the kitchen door. To my left was the restaurant. The bartender, Renata, was cleaning glasses at the far end of the bar. Her back was turned so she couldn't see me.

Otherwise, there were only two people in the restaurant. A tall man with oddly pale skin and white hair sat at the bar, drinking coffee from a little espresso cup. He was dressed entirely in white — white coat, white suit, white shoes.

The other man was Signore del Sarto.

The way they were seated at the bar, they were both looking in my direction. I didn't want them to see me, so I hid behind the suit of armor propped up against the wall of the restaurant and waited for them to go. From where I was standing, I could hear their voices clearly.

"My boss wants his money," the man said to Signore del Sarto. He had a rough Sicilian accent.

Del Sarto lifted his chin haughtily. "I have told him repeatedly —"

"I don't care what you told him," the pale man interrupted. "Now you're talking to me."

"But I explained to him from the beginning that there can be no money until after I have shown the collection! Then the money will flood in."

The pale man stared at him with no emotion at all. He had strange pink eyes. "Now he's changed his mind. He wants the money now."

"Then let him tell me himself."

"*I'm* telling you."

"I don't know who you are," del Sarto said angrily.

"And you don't want to." The man gave Signore del Sarto a hard stare.

Del Sarto's face went white. "You can't threaten me!"

"I can. And I will."

Del Sarto swallowed. "But I must complete my collection! There can be no possibility of money until —"

"Twenty-four hours," the man said. "Then my boss wants his money."

Del Sarto stared at the pale man for a moment. Then something seemed to be dawning on him. He gave the man a bitter smile. "I know who's behind this. It isn't your boss at all." He let out a harsh bark of laughter. "He ruined me once. Now he's doing it again, isn't he?"

The pale man said, "All I know is, you've got twenty-four hours. Or else."

He took out a roll of money from his pocket, peeled off a hundred-euro note, and threw it on the bar next to his tiny cup. Then he stood up and walked out of the restaurant, his white coat swishing as he walked past.

Del Sarto stood and waved his cane at the man. "You tell him he can go —"

But the man was gone before he could finish his sentence.

Signore del Sarto put his face in his hands for a moment. His hands were shaking. Then, abruptly, he stood up and headed for the stairs.

"Whoa!" a voice said, speaking in English. "That was totally cool!"

I turned and saw Brittany. She had been hiding behind a table not more than a couple of meters away from me. She looked around and spotted me. Then her eyes widened a little as she looked at my outfit.

"Wow!" she said. "I *love* your outfit! What happened to the old lady dress?"

"That's my uniform," I said. "My family owns the hotel and I have to wear it when I'm working."

She blinked and stared at me. "You speak English?"

"Sure."

She flushed. "So you heard what I said about you looking like an old lady?"

I nodded.

She looked at the floor. "Sorry about that. Sometimes I get a little carried away with myself." Her embarrassment apparently wore off after about two seconds. "So, look, I'm bored of playing by myself. You want to play with me?"

No, I did not! The last thing in the world that I wanted to do was play with somebody who'd said I looked like an old lady. Even if she did apologize.

But then it hit me. If she had stolen the shoes, the best thing I could do would be to spend time with her.

I shrugged. "Okay," I said. "I'll play with you."

"I'm playing detective," Brittany said. "Did you see that guy in the white suit? It was totally like something out of a *movie*! Let's follow him."

"Follow?"

She didn't wait for an answer. Instead, she hurried down the hallway, leaving the smell of

So Bruno! in her wake. I followed.

We reached the end of the hallway and looked both ways. It was empty.

"Where did he go?" she said.

"To the lobby," I said. I peeked into the lobby. No one in my family was there. Only Aldo, the old bellhop, in his shiny red uniform.

"Hey, excuse me," Brittany called to him in her usual loud voice. "Did you see a guy in a white suit walk through here?"

"I'm sorry," Aldo said in English with a very heavy accent. "I no speak English."

"What's *with* these people?" Brittany said.

I repeated the question in Italian.

Aldo shook his head. "I've been here for ten minutes," he said. "Nobody came through here."

"You sure?"

"I was standing right here. How could I miss him?"

I translated for Brittany. "But that's impossible," she said. "He can't just disappear!"

"I guess Aldo just didn't see him," I said.

Brittany scowled. "Hmph!" she said.

We ran out into the street. The dome of Il Duomo, the famous church, cast a shadow over us. The man in white was gone.

Brittany's eyes glistened. "He must have taken the secret passage!" she said excitedly.

"There is no secret passage," I said.

Brittany poked me on the arm. "Get real," she said. "Look at this place!" She pointed up at the front of the hotel. Somehow seeing it through her eyes made me see it differently. Normally it just seemed like a drab old building to me. But now I saw the ancient stones, the arrow slits, the forbidding tower, the huge wooden front door with its great iron hinges. It seemed suddenly a little bit magical.

"Yes, but —"

"Of *course* it's got a secret passage," Brittany said, hurrying back into the hotel. "Probably tons of them!"

She scampered back into the hallway where we had lost the man in the white clothes. There was nothing there but a broom closet and a row of telephones. Brittany flung open the broom closet door.

"There's probably a false back to this room." She thrust aside a mop and a broom and knocked on the wall. It was obviously solid as a rock. "Hm!" she said.

"I told you," I said.

She sighed heavily, walked into the hallway, and closed the door. "Well, I know it's here." She rapped on the wall with her knuckles, then started poking and prodding the woodwork.

I just stood there with my arms folded. She was a silly girl, but she was kind of funny to watch.

"You know," she said as she continued to search for the secret passage, "I read all about Florence before I came here. Did you know that the noblemen here used to build big castles that looked just like this hotel? They had towers just like this one, too. Sometimes the noblemen would get in fights, and then they'd close all the doors and shoot arrows at each other from the towers."

"This *is* one of those castles," I said.

She turned around and blinked. "You mean it's not a fake?"

"Our hotel is over five hundred years old," I said.

Brittany stared at me. "Five *hundred?*"

I nodded.

"That is totally cool! Then there's definitely a secret passage." She looked around, then sighed again. "I just can't find it."

"There's no secret passage."

"Have it your way," she said lightly.

"So anyway, who's the old guy in the black cape?"

"That's Francesco del Sarto," I said. As though people like him stayed at our hotel all the time.

Brittany's eyes practically bugged out. "*The* Francesco del Sarto?"

I smiled. "Sure."

Brittany put her hands on the side of her face, smashing them together so her mouth formed a little O. "Oh my gosh! Oh my gosh!" She blinked. "Do you suppose he has any of his clothes here? I read in *Vogue* that he's doing his first new collection in twenty years. I would totally *love* to see his new collection!"

I studied her face carefully. Was she pretending not to know that he had his collection in his room to keep me from suspecting that she had stolen the shoes? It didn't look that way. She looked like she'd had no idea that Signore del Sarto's room was stuffed with beautiful clothing.

Which meant I'd been wrong about her.

"You didn't go into his room?" I asked.

Brittany looked at me curiously. "Why? Why would I do that?"

I shrugged. "I'm just asking you. You said you were going to spy on him."

"I mean, I couldn't really. I don't have a key."

"Someone stole his shoes," I said. "Diamond shoes from his new collection."

She narrowed her eyes. "And you thought I —" For a moment she seemed offended. Then she said, "You know what this means don't you?"

"What?"

She dropped her voice to a conspiratorial whisper. "We have to find the shoes!"

"We?" I said.

"I bet it was that guy in the white suit. The evil-looking guy with the pink eyes."

"I don't know," I said. "He didn't say anything about shoes when he talked to Signore del Sarto."

"Something fishy is going on around here."

"Fishy?" I said. "What does fishy mean?"

"A mystery!" she whispered. "There's a mystery! Let's go talk to Signore del Sarto. We'll tell him that we're going to solve the mystery of his disappearing shoes."

"But I'm sure he's very busy."

"Pffff!" Brittany waved her hand. "Who cares? He's got time to talk to *me*."

sette

"Go away!"

Brittany and I were standing in front of Signore del Sarto's door. Brittany looked at me and made a face. "What's his *problem*?" she said. Then she banged on the door again.

"Go away!"

She banged harder. Finally the door flew open. Signore del Sarto stared down at us, eyes narrowed.

"We're here about the shoes," Brittany said in English.

Signore del Sarto stared at her for a moment, then looked at me. "Who is this vulgar little person?" he said to me in Italian. "Her perfume is vile."

"Her name is Brittany," I said. "She's an American. She wants to help you find the diamond shoes."

"*Ridicolo!*" he said. "Tell her to stay outside. Her clothes offend me. And that awful stink is making my eyes water." He grabbed me by the arm and yanked me into the room. "You, however, must come in."

He slammed the door in Brittany's face.

"Del Sarto is rarely wrong," he proclaimed. "But when del Sarto is wrong, he admits it!" He gestured at the dresser's dummy, the one with the gorgeous blue dress. "You were right about the bow. I was wrong. There! You see! Am I such a terrible man? I am not!"

"I told you," I said.

"Yes, but now you have cursed me, you diabolical little genius. Now I shall have to go back and put bows on everything." He sighed theatrically. "It's going to be The Year of the Bow! And it's all your fault."

"I thought you hated bows," I said.

"I detest them! But sometimes a thing becomes unavoidable." He tapped the tiny bow with his cane. "This year the bow will be unavoidable. Milan. Paris. London. New York. It will be everywhere."

Crreeeeeeeeak!

Out of the corner of my eye, I noticed the door opening. Brittany was peering into the room, a funny expression on her face.

"I suppose you'll force me to take you to see the show," he said.

"The show?"

"My collection. I shall arrange tickets for you."

My eyes widened. "Me! You'll let me come to see your fashion show?" I couldn't believe it! It was like a dream come true.

"Of course, you must come!" He pointed one long finger at my face. Then he smiled. It was a very sweet smile. "You have the eye. I can see it. You understand beauty. This is a rare and marvelous thing, my dear."

I grabbed his hand. "Oh, *grazie, grazie, grazie*! Thank you, thank you, thank you!"

"Let's not get carried away," Signore del Sarto said.

Creeeeeeeeeeeeeeeeeak!

As we were talking, Brittany tiptoed into the room, rolling her eyes and making silly faces. Like she thought she was invisible or something. I was afraid she'd mess up my chances of getting to see the fashion show, so I waved frantically at her to get out of the room.

Which was a total waste of time. It was obvious to me by now that Brittany never paid the

slightest attention to what anybody else said.

"I see you, you horribly dressed little child!" del Sarto said, waving his cane at her. "And if I didn't see you, I'd smell you."

Brittany grimaced with irritation. "What's he jabbering about?" she demanded. "Can't you people speak English?"

"Of course I can speak English," Signore del Sarto said. "And sadly—since you have no manners and insist on bursting into my chambers—I suppose I shall be unable to close my ears to whatever nonsense you're about to utter."

"We came to solve the mystery," Brittany said smugly.

"Mystery? Whatever are you talking about?"

"The diamond shoes," she said. "We came to help you get them back."

At the mention of the diamond shoes, del Sarto's face fell. "The shoes. The *shoes!*" he groaned. "Without the shoes, I am lost!"

"C'mon," Brittany said. "One pair of shoes won't make the slightest bit of difference."

"There is where you are wrong," del Sarto said coldly. "They were specially made for Contessa Maria del Forza. The contessa is the most important fashion patron in Florence. She insisted on a pair of diamond shoes. Without them, the ensemble will be incomplete. And that ensemble—that dress *and* the shoes—is the centerpiece, the very *keystone* of my entire collection! Without it, she will tell everyone that the collection is a failure. She will reject me! And if the Contessa turns her face away from me, all of fashion will laugh at me. *I shall be ruined!*"

"Hm," Brittany said. "I guess we really have to find those shoes then, huh?"

Signore del Sarto sat down on the edge of his bed and looked glumly at the blue dress. He didn't answer.

"So who was the man in the white suit?" I asked.

"Just some thug," Signore del Sarto said. He took a deep breath.

"But why did he say you owed him money?" I persisted.

"It's a long story." Del Sarto swept his long hair back with one hand.

"Then you'd better tell us," Brittany said. "It might be connected to the mystery of the missing shoes."

"It all begins twenty-five years ago." He continued to stare at the dress for a while.

Finally he said, "Twenty-five years ago, I hired a young man whose name I will never speak."

"Giancarlo Bruno?" I asked.

"Am I telling the story?" he said sharply. "Or are you?"

"I'm sorry!"

Signore del Sarto continued. "The man whose name I will not speak was a young art student at the time. I hired him to make drawings for me. It soon became clear that he had an enormous talent for design. Perhaps he did not have my genius, my originality. But he had an instinct for how to make a woman look beautiful. And he was, I will freely confess, a far better businessman than me.

"Within a few years, he had become my partner. I trusted him completely. Too much, in fact. Eventually, he stabbed me in the back. Within five years, he controlled the business. But there came a time when we quarreled over matters of design and taste. I am an artist! He only wanted money. So when he got the chance, he simply threw me away like a used rag."

"Everybody knows this," Brittany said.

"What you don't know, vulgar child, is that not only did he get rid of me, but he destroyed my ability to start my own collection. There was a court case. There were contracts. To this day, I still don't understand it all. But not only was I out of the company, my own company, but I was legally prohibited from starting my own line. So I retired to the country. And bided my time. Last year, after twenty years, I finally won my court case against the man whose name I shall not speak."

"Giancarlo Bruno," Brittany said.

"Not another word!" Signore del Sarto shouted. Then his voice dropped. "All of the problems that held me back were gone. I was finally ready. But after twenty years, I was considered a has-been. It costs a lot of money to make a collection. No one would give me the money."

"How much money?" I asked.

"A million euros."

"A million! For some dresses?" I was amazed.

"The dresses are only the beginning. There are models to pay. A hall to rent. Music. Advertising. The list goes on and on. It's all terribly, terribly boring and tedious. But it costs enormous amounts of money."

"So you borrowed the money," Brittany said.

Signore del Sarto nodded. "I borrowed a million euros. From a man of . . . well . . . rather questionable reputation."

"Like a gangster?"

Signore del Sarto shrugged sadly. "I don't know if I'd call him a gangster. But he's not a very nice man, let's put it that way. He told me he would wait until after the show for payment. But now he seems to have changed his mind. He wants a million euros by tomorrow."

"How much is that in real money?" Brittany asked.

"You mean dollars?" I snorted.

"Yeah, dollars."

"More than a million dollars," Signore del Sarto said.

"A million dollars! Whoa!"

"If he knew you had to stage your show and sell the clothes in your collection before you could pay him back, why does he want the money now?"

Del Sarto shook his head. "I think Bruno must have gotten him to do it. Bruno is trying to ruin me again."

"Maybe *he* stole the shoes!" I said.

"I don't think so, my dear. The thing about Bruno is that he never does anything illegal. He never even lies or cheats. He just tricks you. He lets you make a mistake. Then he's on you like a wolf on a rabbit."

"Is there anybody else who might be mad at you?" I asked.

"Mad at me? Of course! Fools are always getting angry at me. That is the curse of being a genius, I'm afraid. One is never understood."

"Specifics." Brittany snapped her finger impatiently. "Names."

Signore del Sarto looked thoughtful. "Hm. You know, I did have a small disagreement with Signore Abruzzi the other day."

"Who's that?" I asked.

"He's my shoemaker. He owns a store near the Ponte Vecchio. In fact, he's the one who made the diamond shoes."

"What did you argue about?"

Signore del Sarto spread his hands. "As I have suggested, money is a . . . difficulty right now. I was unable to pay Signore Abruzzi. I told him, 'No money until I sell the collection.' He became quite abusive and rude. He insisted I give the shoes back to him. Naturally, I refused."

I looked at Brittany. Brittany looked at me.

"Well, *duh!*" Brittany said.

"Duh?" I said. "What does that mean?"

"Duh?" Brittany said. "It's like *duuuuuhhhhhhh!*" She stuck her tongue out of the side of her mouth and crossed her eyes. Suddenly she looked very dumb.

And then I understood exactly what "duh" meant. I started to giggle. "Duhhhh!" I said, making my own stupid face.

Brittany and I started giggling.

"Girls!" Signore del Sarto interrupted. "I'm sure this is all *terribly* entertaining to you. But I am a busy man. Out! Out!" He waved his cane as if he was going to whack us with it.

Brittany and I were still laughing as we hurried toward the door.

"Little girl!" I was halfway out the door as Signore del Sarto's bony hand seized me by the shoulder. This time he was speaking in Italian.

I stopped laughing. "*Si, Signore?*"

"Come to the room again tomorrow at precisely ten o'clock in the morning."

"What for?"

"Your fitting."

I frowned at him, puzzled.

"Your fitting!" the designer repeated, his black eyes boring into me. "I have a dress for you. But it will need to be fitted." He waved his cane at the dresses strewn around his room.

A del Sarto dress? On *me*? It seemed like

magic. Pure joy raced through my veins. For about two seconds.

Then something occurred to me and my mood sank. He wouldn't just *give* me a dress. And my parents could never afford to pay for a del Sarto original. "I'm not sure that my parents would allow —" I started.

"Be here at 10."

Signore del Sarto shoved me out the door and slammed it behind us. I stumbled into the hallway, eyes wide. I was going to have a real del Sarto dress! Fitted by Francesco del Sarto *himself*! It seemed impossible.

Brittany grabbed my hand and dragged me down the hallway. "Where's this Ponti Vecko place?"

"Ponte Vecchio," I said. "It's a famous bridge over the Arno River."

"Is it near here?"

"Yes but —"

She looked impatient. "Then let's go!"

"I can't," I said. "I'll get in trouble. I'm supposed to be in my room."

But I couldn't stop myself from trying to find the shoes. Next thing I knew, we were at the Ponte Vecchio.

otto

The Ponte Vecchio is the oldest bridge in Florence. It was built across the Arno River more than 650 years ago. It actually has buildings built right on the bridge—old workshops with stucco walls and red tiled roofs. When it was first built, there were butchers and blacksmiths and all kinds of shops on the bridge. But the duke who lived nearby thought they made too much noise. So in 1593 he kicked them all out and rented all the shops to jewelry makers. It's been that way ever since.

Because of the jewelry shops, the area around the Ponte Vecchio has become a good place to buy fancy things — or to have fancy things made for you. Just across the bridge we found a small house with a shoe painted on the window. *Antonio Abruzzi, Shoemaker,* it said. If you blinked your eyes when you were walking by, you would miss it. Behind the dusty window was a jumble of the most beautiful shoes I'd ever seen.

"What do we do now?" I said.

Brittany didn't answer. She just pushed open the door and walked in. A small bell tinkled as I followed her in.

The smell of leather surrounded us. The shop was tiny, about the size of a bathroom. There was a counter in the back, but the room was empty.

"Hello!" Brittany called out in English. "Hey! Anybody here?"

There was no answer.

"What are you doing?" I whispered.

"I have an idea!" she whispered back. Then, loudly: "Hello! Excuse me! Hello! What's the deal here?"

After a moment, a small, thin-faced man with a missing front tooth came to the door at the back of the tiny shop. Signore Abruzzi, presumably. When he saw that we were kids, he scowled. "Out!" he snapped in Italian. "No children."

"What'd he say?"

"No children," I translated. "I guess we'd better go."

"Pff!" Brittany said. She opened her Bruno purse and took out a Bruno wallet, from which she extracted a gold credit card. "Tell him I'm a totally spoiled rich girl from New York and I want to buy a pair of shoes. Tell him my Daddy gives me a credit card and I can buy anything I want."

"Yeah but —"

"Hey, it's *true!*" she said. "Just tell him."

"Okay," I said. Then I turned to the man and started to explain in Italian.

He cut me off. "I don't make shoes for children," he said. "Out."

Then he disappeared.

"Oh, well," I said. "We tried." I started to turn for the door.

But Brittany didn't seem fazed. There was a hinged section of the wooden counter that you could flip up to walk through. She pushed it up and barged into the back room. It was a cramped workshop full of worn tools and beautiful pieces of leather.

Signore Abruzzi was sitting at a workbench. In front of him were a pair of half-made, red leather shoes. He was poking a needle-sharp awl through the leather.

"Tell this guy I'm gonna spend a ton of money and it would be dumb not to take it," Brittany said.

He looked up at me and said, "Tell this rude little American that her papa doesn't have enough money to make me sit here smelling her perfume all afternoon." It was obvious he spoke English, but he didn't feel like talking to Brittany.

"I want something very special, Mr. Abruzzi," Brittany said. "A pair of blue shoes. Pale blue. Pumps. With a diamond on each one."

Signore Abruzzi slammed the awl down into the wooden workbench. "No children!" he shouted.

"She just wants shoes!" I said desperately.

"I'll pay you 20,000 euros," Brittany said. "But they have to be *very* special shoes."

"Out."

Brittany held out her gold card. "Here. Run the card. Twenty thousand euros."

"You can't be serious!" I hissed. "Your papa will kill you!"

Brittany shrugged. "Twenty thousand," she said again.

The shoemaker took the credit card and scrutinized it carefully, front and back. Then he threw it down. "I do not have such a pair of shoes," he said in English.

"Then make them," Brittany said.

The shoemaker's eyes narrowed. "Who sent you?" the shoemaker demanded. "Did del Sarto send you?"

"Make me a pair of shoes!" Brittany stomped her foot.

The shoemaker just stared at her.

Suddenly Brittany's face collapsed and a line of big, fat tears started rolling out of her eyes. "I just want some shoes!" she wailed. "Please! Mr. del Sarto said you're the best!" As she covered her face with her hands, she gave me a mischievous smile. It was an impressive performance. Tears and everything!

The shoemaker looked uncomfortably at me. "Look, tell her I can't do what she asks. Those shoes I made for del Sarto, they are *couture* shoes. You make them one time and you're done. If I steal that design, my reputation would be ruined. I would never sell another shoe again."

Brittany wiped her eyes and gave me a pitiful look. "What's he saying?"

"He says he can't make the shoes."

She blotted her eyes, looked at him slyly. "Then maybe you have the originals?"

Signore Abruzzi looked puzzled. "Signore del Sarto has the shoes," he said in English.

I shook my head.

The shoemaker's eyes widened. "Someone stole them?"

I nodded.

"Oh, no," he said. "Now I'll never get paid!" He sighed loudly. "I had to take money out of my savings to buy the diamonds."

"Oh," I said. "I'm sorry."

The shoemaker stared at the unfinished shoe in front of him. "So del Sarto sent you to see if I stole them?"

"No!" I said. "We're just trying to find them ourselves. He said you had a fight over money. He said you told him you were going to take back the shoes if he didn't pay you."

Signore Abruzzi shook his head glumly. "Del Sarto promised me I'd be paid half the money after I finished the shoes. Then, of course, he didn't have the money. So I shouted at him. It's the only way to deal with the man. If he weren't so brilliant . . ." He shrugged. "But he is brilliant. So what can you do?"

"So you really don't have the diamond shoes?" I asked.

"No diamond shoes."

"We better go," I said nervously. "Papa's going to kill me if he finds out I snuck out of the house."

As we headed back to the hotel, I asked, "Would your papa really let you spend 20,000 euros on a pair of shoes?"

Brittany grinned mischievously. "Duh! Of course not!"

We both burst out laughing.

CHAPTER NINE

nove

I had just snuck back to my room and sat down on the bed when I heard the door to our apartment open.

"Gia!"

I was sure I was going to be in trouble. *Big* trouble. I was sure my parents would know I'd gone.

"Gia!" Mama opened the door to my room. "I hope that sitting here in your room for the past two hours has given you a little time to think about what you did."

Sitting here in my room for the past two hours? So they must not know. I felt a huge burst of relief.

Mama came in and closed the door.

"Gia," she said softly, "I know why you did what you did."

"You *do*?" I said.

Mama is a tall, beautiful woman with long brown hair that she usually keeps wrapped up around her head. Most of the time she seems happy. But sometimes when she thinks nobody is looking, she seems very sad. And I've never known why.

Mama sat down on my bed and ran her fingers through my hair. "When I was a little girl," she said, "I wanted to be an artist. I used to draw all the time. But we didn't have any money. So I couldn't afford to go to art school. I came to work here when your grandfather and grandmother still ran the hotel. I was intending to save up enough money so I could study art in Paris. But then your father and I fell in love." She shrugged. "And that was the end of my dream of becoming an artist."

I knew Mama loved beautiful things. But I never knew she wanted to be an artist.

"Your father loves this hotel. It means everything to him. Me?" She shrugged. "Me, I love your father. But not the hotel."

I wasn't really sure what she was getting at.

"Gia, when you grow up, I don't want you working in this hotel. Cristina is like your father; she'll take care of this place. But I want you to do something you love."

"That's why I went into Signore del Sarto's room!" I said. "I couldn't help myself!"

"I understand that," Mama said. "But you must remember that this is not a playground. It's a hotel. You can't go into a room and touch things. When you do that, it's not just you who suffers. It hurts your father. It hurts Cristina. It hurts the hotel."

I don't know why, but suddenly I felt tears stinging my eyes.

"I don't care about the hotel!" I said.

"Do you care about your father?" she asked.

I nodded.

"Then you understand why you can never, never, never do anything like that again."

Mama kept stroking my hair without saying anything.

Finally she spoke. "Your father and I have discussed it. You're grounded. Other than school, you can't leave the hotel for the next two weeks."

I sat up. "No!" I shouted.

Mama pressed her lips together. "I'm sorry, *bambina*. Two weeks."

I felt sick. "But Mama! Signore del Sarto asked me to go to his fashion show tomorrow."

She frowned. "I'm sure he didn't mean it," she said.

"He did, Mama," I moaned. "He wants me

to come up to his room at ten o'clock tomorrow morning. He's going to fit a dress on me."

Mama squinted at me, then cocked her head. "He *what*?"

"I'm serious! He's going to fit me with a dress! He wants me to go to his show tomorrow."

Mama suddenly looked mad. "Come with me, young lady," she said. "I'm going to have a conversation with that man."

I followed her out the door. She marched out of the apartment, through the kitchen, and into the hotel. Within a minute or two we were standing in front of del Sarto's room. Mama was banging on the door with her fist.

The door opened a crack. "What?" demanded Signore del Sarto.

"I am Signora Russo. This is my daughter Gia!"

"And — ?"

"What do you mean by torturing her like this?"

"I?" He raised one eyebrow.

"She made a mistake. She is being punished for it. That does not give you the right to make promises you have no intention of keeping."

Signore del Sarto looked confused. "I'm afraid

I don't understand, Signora."

"Promising her a dress?" Mama's cheeks were hot. "Promising her she could go to see your collection? It's spiteful and disgusting."

Signore del Sarto opened the door slowly. On the far side of the room, a small powder blue dress hung from a hanger. "There is her dress, Signora," he said quietly.

Mama stared at it. I stared, too. It was beautiful. It had little beads hanging off the bottom, like an old dress from the 1920s. It even had a bow on it. In precisely the same place as the one I'd put on the other dress. I could hardly breathe.

"But," Mama said. "We could never afford —"

"Signora, your daughter is both lovely and talented. She deserves to be seen in the dress. I am not giving it to her. I am simply inviting her to come to the show, where she will wear the dress. She will then return it to me."

Mama kept staring at the dress. Her face was wistful. "Really?" she said. "You mean it?"

"I never lie," del Sarto said, lifting his chin.

Mama's face hardened. "Well, I will have to be here for the fitting," she said sharply. "It's quite inappropriate for a young girl to be fitted by herself."

"That goes without saying, Signora," Signore del Sarto said. "Ten o'clock."

Then he slammed the door in our faces.

Mama looked at me strangely. "Well, he's not a very polite man, is he?" she said.

"No."

She sighed. "Oh, but he makes such gorgeous dresses."

I nodded. Was it really going to happen? Was it possible? I felt like I was standing at the edge of a very high diving board, waiting to plunge into the distant water.

Suddenly Mama started laughing. She grabbed me and gave me a hug. "You're going to a fashion show!" she whispered.

CHAPTER TEN

✪

dieci

"Absolutely not!"

When you work in a hotel, dinnertime is always late. Because it was Fashion Week, the hotel was stuffed with people, and the restaurant stayed open even later than usual. We had finally sat down to dinner. My father insists that no matter how late he works, we all sit down to dinner together and eat a properly prepared meal. Linen napkins, china, wine for him and Mama.

My father had led the prayers, then served the food. Then— finally—Mama had told him about the fashion show.

Papa slammed his fist on the table. The plates jumped up in the air. Papa's bread fell on the floor. "Absolutely, absolutely not!"

I looked at Mama, stricken.

"Young lady," Papa said to me, "you betrayed the trust of a guest. You went into his room and you touched his clothes." He picked up his spoon and took a sip of the *zuppa*.

"But he was glad!" I said. "He *liked* the bow I put on his dress. He said that this year —just because of me — the bow is going to be as unavoidable as —"

"I said *no*!" His whole face was red. Soup sprayed from his mouth.

"Alberto," Mama said softly, "this is a once-in-a-lifetime chance."

Papa thumped his chest. "We are hoteliers. That is what we are. Simple, honest, hard-working people. We are not . . . not . . . not . . ." He seemed unable to find the words. "We are not foolish little people who wear capes and wave silver canes around. We are not people who waste our lives fussing around with bows and ribbons."

"Alberto —" Mama said softly.

"I'm not finished, Antonia! We make beds. We clean rooms. We pay attention to little things. And because of this, our guests feel safe and respected and clean and carefree. We are not ashamed of what we do! We are proud!"

Mama's lower lip trembled. She didn't speak.

"It's only setting her up for disappointment!" Papa gestured at me with his soup spoon. "What good is it to dangle things in front of her that she will never be able to have?" He waved his spoon

in a big circle, taking in the room with its low and ancient timbered ceiling, the old stove, the dim lights, the worn furniture. "This is who we are!"

Mama looked at him for a long time.

When she finally spoke, her voice was barely louder than a whisper. "It is who *you* are."

She set her linen napkin gently on the table. Then she stood up and walked swiftly out of the room.

Papa stared at the doorway. "Antonia!" he called. "Wait a minute! Antonia, come back here!"

He flung his napkin down and rushed out of the room.

Cristina gave me a venomous look. "Gia's so *beautiful*," she said sarcastically. "Gia has such *fashion sense*. Every time I turn around I hear, 'Gia this, Gia that.' I'm so sick of hearing it."

"What's wrong with wanting to wear beautiful clothes?" I asked. "Is that a crime?"

"I do *all* the work around here. I do everything right. I work so hard. And nobody cares about me at all."

"What are you talking about? *I'm* the one who's always in trouble because I did everything wrong."

Cristina gave me a level look, then scooped up a big spoonful of pasta and heaped it on her plate. "You're just a spoiled, lazy little girl who gets a free pass because you're pretty," she said, cramming a big portion of it into her mouth. She gave me a big, angry smile, pasta sticking out of her teeth. "But one day you'll see. Pretty goes away like that." She snapped her fingers.

CHAPTER ELEVEN

undici

I didn't sleep at all that night. I just kept staring up at the crack on the ceiling above my bed, the same questions turning over and over in my brain.

Who stole the diamond shoes? And how did they do it? Did someone pick the lock? Did someone steal the key? How did the man in white disappear in the middle of our hotel?

He seemed to be the key. Maybe he stole the shoes. Maybe he hid them somewhere. If I could figure out how he disappeared, maybe I could find some answers.

Suddenly I sat up, eyes wide.

The wine cellar! What if the man in the white clothes got out through the wine cellar somehow?

I got slowly, quietly out of bed. On the other side of the room, Cristina breathed heavily and flopped over in the bed. Thump! I froze, my heart in my throat.

After a minute, her breathing evened out. I slowly put my clothes on. When I was dressed,

I grabbed Cristina's flashlight, snuck out the door, down the hallway, and out of our apartment.

Nobody heard me.

I headed upstairs. It was amazing how quiet the hotel was at night. It was like a tomb. Soon I was standing in front of Brittany's room. Most kids who came to our hotel shared a room with their parents. Not Brittany, of course. She had her own room.

I knocked softly on the door.

"Who is it?" a small voice asked after a while.

"It's Gia," I whispered.

She opened the door and looked at me, puzzled and squinting. Her hair stuck up in all directions and she was holding a small, worn teddy bear. When she noticed me looking at the bear, she said, "I can't help it. I love him. His name's Brown Dog."

"Dog?" I was thinking I was getting confused between the words in English—dog and bear.

"I was three when I got him," she said. "I insisted he was a dog." She patted down her hair a little. "So, why are you here?"

"Get your clothes on," I said. "I'll explain on the way."

A few minutes later we were walking through the restaurant kitchen. In the back was a large, heavy door with old wrought-iron hinges and an old-fashioned lock. The key hung on a rusty nail on the wall.

"Okay, where are we going?" Brittany asked loudly.

"Shhh!" I pointed at the wall. We were right next door to our family's apartment. I could feel my blood beating through my body. I knew if Papa heard us sneaking around here, he'd kill me. He was already mad enough at me as it was.

I unlocked the door and opened it slowly. It groaned on its hinges, revealing a set of stone stairs leading down into blackness.

"Cool!" Brittany whispered. "What is this place?"

"It's the wine cellar," I whispered, turning on my flashlight.

The battery was not as strong as I would have liked. It threw a dim yellow circle of light onto the stairs in front of me as I slowly descended into the dark. Brittany followed.

"Don't they have lights down here?" she asked.

"No," I said. "We always use a flashlight."

"Man, this is spooky!"

She was right. It *was* spooky. I realized I had

never come down here by myself before. Only with Papa. I could hear a soft drip of water. Otherwise, it was completely silent. Silent like nothing I had ever heard before.

We got to the bottom of the stairs and I waved my light around. Above us was a low, vaulted roof of stone. It was smudged and blackened with soot and coated with cobwebs. Rows of wine racks stood against one wall, along with boxes full of Orangina and Coca-Cola.

"You could probably scream your head off and nobody would hear you down here," Brittany said.

"Papa says it's even older than the hotel," I said. "This building was built as a sort of castle by a famous family in 1523. But there was an older building here before."

"Even *older*?"

"Yes." I shined my dim light around the cellar. The walls were black and water-stained. "The people who owned it were famous noblemen, the Renaldis. They had huge parties here and wore beautiful clothes. There were musicians and painters and artists here all the time. The Renaldis were great patrons of the arts. Supposedly, the castle was decorated by the greatest artists of the time—Michelangelo, Raphael, Leonardo."

"Wow!" Brittany said. "I thought the house *I* live in is old. It was built like 75 years ago."

I kept going with my story. "Like you had said earlier, the noblemen in Florence back then were always getting into fights with each other. That's why they built the towers and the heavy doors and the arrow slits. So anyway, the Renaldis, they got in a feud with another family, the di Cristofanos. The di Cristofanos were terrible people. They didn't care about beautiful things or music or dancing or painting."

Brittany pulled a bottle of wine off the rack, blew the dust off it, and examined the label. "Whoa," she said, "this bottle of wine is older than my *house!*"

"The feud lasted for almost two generations," I continued. "The Renaldis and di Cristofanos were killing each other one by one. For almost fifty years nobody from either family could go out at night for fear of being attacked. Finally the Renaldis said, 'This is crazy.' So they got together with the di Cristofanos and they proposed a way to stop fighting. The di Cristofanos said okay. Eventually they signed a contract and it was agreed that the youngest son of the Renaldis would marry the youngest daughter of the di Cristofanos. But it was all a trick. The night before the wedding, the di Cristofanos snuck into the Renaldi's villa and murdered everybody. Even the children. Then the di Cristofanos's knocked down the building. Every last stone. Except for the cellar. They said, 'After this, the Renaldis will be forgotten forever.' Then they built their own castle on top of the cellar."

"Maybe there are ghosts!" Brittany said. "Mwaaaaaa haaaa haaa haaaaaaaa!"

It was silly, but her ghost laugh made the hair on the back of my neck stand up.

I walked back past the wine racks and the stacks of soft drinks until I found what I was looking for. It was a place where the stones were replaced by brick. There had obviously been a door here. But it had been bricked up long, long ago.

At the bottom of the brick wall was a small, roughly made hole.

"You're not serious," Brittany said.

"You wanted a secret passage," I said.

Brittany's face was barely visible in the light, her eyes hidden in blackness. "But I was thinking like you pressed on a secret panel and a bookshelf would turn around or something."

"Papa told me this is how the di Cristofanos got into the house all those years ago."

"Where does it go?"

"I don't know."

"You've never gone through it?"

I shook my head. "I had forgotten it was here. But then you were talking about a secret tunnel. And then I thought about that man in the white clothes disappearing. Where could he have gone?" I pointed at the hole. "Maybe he went through here."

"Yeah but —"

"If we find out where it goes," I said, "we might be able to find out where he came from. Maybe whoever sent him is the same person who stole the shoes. Maybe *he* stole them."

"I'm not going in there," Brittany said nervously.

"It's just a little hole," I said. "There has to be a room or passage on the other side. No problem."

Brittany didn't say anything for a minute. "I'm claustrophobic," she said.

"What does that mean?"

"I'm scared of small places." Suddenly she started shivering. Shivering so hard her teeth started clicking together.

"We have to find those shoes," I said.

"I can't," Brittany said.

"Sure you can." I stooped down and stuck my flashlight into the hole. A cool draft blew up. The light seemed to simply disappear into the blackness. "Follow me," I told her.

Then I started crawling. I was sure I would come out the other side in a foot or two. But then, as soon as I got inside, I realized I was wrong. The hole—which was only a little wider than my shoulders and just high enough for me to crawl through—kept going as far as my flashlight's beam could point.

"Wait!" Brittany's voice was a high wail. "Wait! Don't leave me in the dark."

Now *I* was scared. I felt like I was stuck in a tight box. Brittany scrambled into the hole behind me. I couldn't back up, so I had no choice but to move forward. I began crawling.

"Wait! Please!" Brittany said. She was breathing fast and loud.

"It's okay," I said. "Just follow me." I tried to sound braver than I felt. All I could think was, *This was a dumb idea!*

But I couldn't back up. As I crawled forward, the tiny passage began to get even narrower. Rocks poked out of the wall, pressing into my arms and my back. Cobwebs hung in my face. I swung

my flashlight in front of my face, knocking the cobwebs aside. I hate spiders. *Hate* them! This was the scariest thing I'd ever done in my life. My heart was beating faster and faster.

And the further I went, the tighter it got.

Behind me, Brittany was moaning softly. "I can't do this! I can't do this!"

"We're almost there," I said, though, truthfully, I couldn't see anything in front of me.

A thought hit me. *What if the passage just ended?* Backing up would be a lot harder than going forward. What if we got stuck? My arms and legs were starting to feel weak and shaky.

Keep going, Gia! I thought. *Just keep going!*

I forced myself to go forward. Centimeter by painful centimeter.

The rocks closed in until finally I couldn't crawl. I had to squirm forward like a snake. More cobwebs.

I swung wildly at the cobwebs with the flashlight. The flashlight smashed on the rocks.

And went out.

We were in total, complete darkness. For a moment, I couldn't even move.

"Gia?" I heard a tiny, plaintive voice behind me. "Gia? Where's the light? Gia!"

"It went out," I said.

"Help!" Brittany screamed. "Somebody! *Help!*"

But the rock just seemed to swallow the sound of her voice.

I switched the flashlight off and on repeatedly. Nothing.

"What are we gonna do? Gia?" Brittany's voice was high and whispery and desperate.

I took a deep breath. "We have to keep going," I said.

"I can't," came her tiny voice.

"You have to," I said. Then I began squirming forward.

Cobwebs brushed against my face. I imagined spiders crawling all around me. I was shaking and my heart was about to thump out of my chest.

But I kept moving. "You can do it, Brittany," I said. "We're almost there."

"You keep saying that!" she cried.

And then, suddenly, the passage got a lot bigger. I was able to get to my knees again! I crawled forward. The rock fell away from me now. We were finally coming out!

"We're here!" I shouted. "We made it!"

And then the rock beneath me gave way and I fell into the blackness.

CHAPTER TWELVE

⟡

dodici

I hit the ground with a solid thump that made me see stars. When the stars faded, though, it was just as dark as ever.

I could hear Brittany above me somewhere, scrambling around.

"Look out!" I called. "There's a —"

She crashed on top of me.

"Ow!" she said.

I pushed her off of me, then fumbled around, feeling for my flashlight. My hands hit the light. I picked it up and tried the switch, but it still didn't work. I whacked it with my palm, and the dim light came on.

Brittany was still lying on the floor. Her whole body was shaking.

"Are you okay?" I asked.

"I can't stand up," she said.

"Are you hurt?"

She shook her head. "I'm just scared!" she said. "My legs are like rubber." Then she started laughing, a strange, hysterical laugh. She rolled around on the ground, got slowly to her knees, then fell down again. She kept laughing. Finally she stood up, her legs still wobbly. She held onto the wall. "Oh, my gosh," she said. "There better be another way out, 'cause I'm not going through that hole again."

I shined the light around us. We were in a large chamber. It had a marble floor and marble walls. Except for the fact that it didn't have any windows, it didn't seem like a cellar at all. There were torches hanging from the walls.

"I wonder if we could light those torches," I said. "My flashlight is not so good."

Brittany opened her Bruno purse, which was now scuffed and dirty. She came out with a pack of matches. "Try these. I always take matches when we go to a restaurant. I collect 'em."

I took the pack of matches, struck one, and held it up to one of the torches. It sputtered, then lit, with a smell of burning pine trees.

"Wow," Brittany said. "I wonder how old that torch is."

"It could be 500 years old," I said.

I lifted the torch off the wall and circled the room, lighting all the torches, one after another.

Soon the entire room was brightly lit. On the far side of the room was a doorway leading into a dark passage. Fortunately, this one was much larger than the one we'd just crawled through.

"Let's see where it goes," I said.

But Brittany didn't move. She was staring up in the air.

"Is something wrong?" I asked.

"Oh my gosh!" she said.

"What?"

She just pointed straight up in the air.

I raised the torch and looked up. And there, above us, was a high arched ceiling. Painted on it was an enormous, breathtakingly beautiful painting. It looked like a picture of a big party. There were beautiful women wearing richly decorated clothes. The sort of clothes that people wore in the 1500s. There were men wearing brightly colored outfits with swords thrust through belts. There were jugglers and clowns and musicians playing lutes. Everyone was laughing.

I just stared. In the far corner was a painted pedestal with an M at the bottom. I knew that M. Every schoolgirl and schoolboy in Florence knew it. It was the signature used by the most famous artist ever to live in Florence. Maybe the most

famous artist of all time.

"Michelangelo!" I whispered.

For a moment, we just stared.

And then we heard something, a dull and ominous boom in the distance.

"What was that?" Brittany asked.

I shook my head. "We'd better go," I said.

Brittany grabbed a torch off the wall. We ran through the door at the far end of the chamber and found ourselves in a long stone hallway with an arched ceiling. It continued for a while, then turned left and branched in three directions. We ran down the first hallway to the right. Eventually it came to a blank wall and stopped. It looked as if someone had closed it off at the end because there was a different, rougher-looking stone.

"Oh, man," Brittany wailed. "There better be a way out. I don't think I can go through that again."

We ran back and tried another hallway. But this one, too, led nowhere. The tunnel simply ended, stopping at a large rock. It was as though the builders had hit a boulder and just quit. We ran back yet again and tried the third and last hallway.

This one turned twice. Then, finally, it ended. But this one wasn't sealed shut. Instead, a huge wooden door blocked our way. There was no lock, but a thick wrought-iron bolt held it closed.

I pulled on the bolt, expecting it to be rusted shut. But instead, it moved easily. Like someone had just oiled it.

We found ourselves in a dark room. It was a basement. But it was obviously the basement of a much more modern building. There was a concrete floor. And over our heads I could see steel beams holding up the ceiling.

At the far end of the room was another door. A modern steel door with a modern lock.

We walked over, exchanged glances, then Brittany pulled open the door. It led to a dim stairway.

"I guess I better not walk up into this building carrying a lighted torch!" Brittany said, giggling. She stubbed out the flame in the dirt floor, then we headed up the steps. When we got to the top, we found ourselves in a small room. Filled with boxes and cans, it looked like the back room of a small grocery store. At the far end of the room, four men were seated at a table. Two of them were playing chess. The other two were watching. They all turned and looked at us. This must have been how the man got into and out of our hotel. But if it was, how did he keep his clothes so white?

"Uh-oh!" I said. One of the men was the man in white. He saw me from across the room with his pale, pink eyes.

Before we could make it down the stairs, one of the men across the room stopped us.

"Let go of me!" Brittany shouted. "I'll sue! I'm an American! I want my lawyer!"

The pale man ignored her and dragged us back to the table where he'd been sitting. A short, fat man with what was obviously a toupee on his head looked at us with amusement.

"Little past your bedtime, isn't it, girls?"

I smiled weakly.

"Who are you?" the man demanded. "What are you doing in my building?"

"My name is Gia Russo," I said. "My family owns the Pensione Russo."

The man smiled. "Oh, yeah, yeah," he said. "I know the place. This shop we're in is connected to the back of your hotel." Then he frowned. "Nicola, you were over there today, huh?"

"Yeah, boss, I was." He eyed me for a minute. "Matter of fact, I saw these two little sneaks spying on me when I was having my little chat with our friend del Sarto."

The boss had a way of smiling where his lips moved but his eyes seemed dead. "Spying!" he said. "Isn't that cute." He reached out and gave my cheek a little pinch. "How come you're spying on Nicola, girls?"

"We were just playing," I said.

He laughed loudly. "Yeah. And you girls just snuck into my basement by accident, too."

We were speaking Italian and Brittany couldn't understand anything we were saying, so she just sat there staring.

"It's true!" I said.

"Go stick these kids in a room somewhere, Nicola," the boss said. "I need to figure out what to do with 'em."

"Okay, okay, wait!" I said. I figured there was no harm in telling the truth. "We're looking for shoes."

"Shoes," the boss said.

"A pair of shoes was stolen from Signore del Sarto. We thought that maybe . . . uh . . . this gentleman here found them. Or something."

"Found them? Found like *found*? Or found like *stole*?"

"Okay, stole," I said. "We thought maybe he stole them."

"What do they look like?"

"Blue. Blue with diamonds."

"Did you steal the shoes from del Sarto?" the boss asked the pale man.

The pale man shook his head, then looked at me like I was an idiot. "What would I want with a pair of girl's shoes?"

"I thought maybe you were trying to scare him or something," I said.

"Scare him?" the pale man said sarcastically. He made a fist and waved it in my face.

"If I want to scare him, I'll give him a little taste of this."

"So then why are you mad at Signore del Sarto?" I asked.

"Mad?" the boss laughed. "I'm not mad."

"But — this man threatened him," I said.

"I'm sort of a banker," the man said.

"Someone needs money and he can't get it from a regular bank, he comes to me."

"So you're a loan shark," I said.

"Hey," the man shrugged, "that's a very negative word. Hurts my feelings." He didn't look like his feelings were hurt.

"Then you don't know anything about the shoes, sir?"

"I'm telling you, kid," the boss said. "I loaned that old clown some money. I want him to pay it back. With interest. A lot of interest. Now how am I gonna get paid back if I steal all the stuff he's supposed to be selling at his fashion show? Explain that to me, kid."

I didn't have an answer.

"What are they saying?" Brittany asked.

I explained what the boss had said.

She looked thoughtful. "It makes sense," she said. "He'd have no reason to steal the shoes if he wants his money."

"So why did your man threaten Signore del Sarto?" I asked the boss.

"Part of my business," the man said. "I gotta impress on people the importance of paying me back. A guy like this del Sarto, you gotta throw a scare in him every now and then. It's part of the business."

"Can we just go now?" I said. "We just came here to look for the shoes."

The boss looked up at the pale man. "Get rid of 'em," he said.

I felt my knees get weak. *No!* I thought.

The boss winked at me. "Hey, I'm just kidding, *bambina.*"

Relief rushed through my veins like a jolt of ice water.

The boss nodded at the pale man. "Walk these crazy girls back to the hotel. Lotta bad people on the streets this time of night. Be terrible if something happened to a couple of sweet girls like this."

tredici

At precisely 10 o'clock the next morning, I was standing in front of Signore del Sarto's room. Mama had finally convinced Papa to let me get the dress fitted. He still hadn't made up his mind about letting me go to the fashion show. But I figured if he was going to let me get the dress, he would let me go to the fashion show.

Signore del Sarto opened the door. "Ah, my dear," he said, "come in! Signora Russo, come in!"

He fussed over us both, brought Mama some biscotti and coffee, and some Swiss chocolate for me. Then, finally, he brought out the dress. It was even more beautiful than I remembered. The beads glittered and caught the sunlight from the window.

I have to admit the fitting process was not that much fun. I stood on top of a trunk while he circled around me, a little pincushion attached to his wrist. He pinned here and there, making tiny adjustments in the fit. Sometimes he would make little marks on the fabric with a white pencil.

After about two minutes, it seemed fine.

But Signore del Sarto was not easily satisfied. He kept pinning and marking, frowning and fussing. It was kind of strange, being stared at like that. Was I too fat or too tall or too thin or too *something* for his dress? I suppose he was just looking at the dress. And after awhile, my feet hurt.

Finally, Signore del Sarto stepped back. "Hmm," he said skeptically. "What do you think, Signora Russo?"

Before Mama could answer, there was a loud knock on the door.

"Francesco!" a voice called. "Francesco, I am here!" It was a woman's voice.

Signore del Sarto's face went white. "Oh no!" he said.

"Who is it?" I asked.

"Don't answer it!" he said.

"Why not?"

"It's Contessa del Forza!" he whispered. "She'll want to see the dress." He swallowed. "And the shoes."

"Francesco! Answer this door immediately. I know you're in there!"

Signore del Sarto seemed frozen to the floor.

"Open up!" More banging. "You can't hide from me!"

Signore del Sarto took a deep breath, swept back his long black hair, and opened the door. "Ah, Contessa!" he said. "Look at you!"

The Contessa was a wiry woman, perfectly dressed, with a face that would have been extraordinarily beautiful if she hadn't had a very thin, somewhat cruel mouth. It was almost as if she had no lips at all. Her hair was a glossy white with a streak of black running above one ear.

The Contessa stepped forward, kissed Signore del Sarto on both cheeks, and entered the room as though walking onto a stage. She ignored Mama and stared straight at me. Well, probably at the dress.

"My goodness!" she said. "You are surprising! *Magnifico!*" She circled, touching the dress here and there. "The details . . . superb! The balance . . . marvelous! The execution . . . perfect!" Then she narrowed her eyes, reached out, and touched the bow on my chest. She cocked her head slightly and her cruel smile faded. "And what is this?"

"It is a bow, Contessa," del Sarto said. "Perhaps you have heard of them?"

The Contessa turned and looked at the designer. "I once recall you saying terrible things about bows. You offended me deeply."

"It is The Year of the Bow, Contessa," Signore del Sarto said lightly. "They will be quite unavoidable this year."

"Really?" The Contessa seemed unconvinced.

"Del Sarto has spoken." The designer lifted his chin. "Therefore, it is so!"

"Bows," she said. "Hmm, perhaps you're right."

Signore del Sarto winked at me. I grinned back at him.

"Well," the Contessa said, "you know very well why I am here."

Del Sarto looked puzzled. "Do I?"

"The dress, you fool," she said.

"Which dress was that?"

Contessa del Forza looked at me. "He thinks he's being humorous. But I find him quite tedious. Don't you, my dear?"

I didn't know what to say.

She didn't seem to expect me to say anything, though. She clapped her hands together sharply. "Bring out the ensemble, Francesco."

Del Sarto waved his cane in the air. "Oh, *that* dress."

"*Now,* Francesco." Contessa del Forza looked at him coldly.

Del Sarto shook his head. "No, no, no, no, Contessa. It's simply not possible."

"I demand it!" she said, gritting her teeth.

Del Sarto shrugged and smiled slightly. "No."

She blinked and stared at him. She obviously couldn't believe he was refusing her. "I think I don't need to remind you," she said, "that your entire future rides upon my good opinion."

Del Sarto looked at her as though he found her amusing. "My dear, your dress is far too important to unveil in such modest surroundings. It is a major, major dress. I'm a little shocked, frankly, that you would put me in such an embarrassing position. It really shows a terrible lack of taste on your part." He smiled. "No offense intended, my dear."

Her black eyes met his. "You refuse me," she said.

"I do," he said lightly. "And tonight when you see the dress, when you see the shoes, in their appropriate setting, you will thank me for not ruining the moment here. It will be a glorious moment for you. Don't spoil it. I beg you."

She studied his face for a very long time.

The room was silent. Nobody moved.

"You're hiding something," she said finally.

Signore del Sarto laughed. "Only my genius," he said. "Only my genius."

Suddenly she whirled and headed to the door. Then she stopped and said, "If there is a single flaw, a single button out of place, a single thing missing —" she pointed her finger, "— then I will devastate you."

"Such a thing is impossible," Signore del Sarto said.

She continued to glare at him. Then her face

softened slightly and her eyes turned to me. "Your young model is really quite stunning. Who is she?"

"It's Gia," Signore del Sarto said. "I'm terribly surprised you haven't seen her before." He gave another wink in my direction.

I couldn't believe it! Contessa del Forza, the most important fashion patron in Florence, had just called me *stunning*. I felt a rush of happiness.

"Tonight everything had better be perfect," the Contessa said again. Then she walked out, slamming the door behind her.

Signore del Sarto fell backward onto the bed as if all the life had drained out of him. "Oh, no!" he said. "What am I going to do? I *must* find those shoes!"

Something struck me then. "I talked to a man yesterday who said that if we wanted to figure out who stole the shoes, we should find out who most wanted to do you harm."

Signore del Sarto just lay on the bed, staring up in the air. "I'm ruined," he said.

"Who would want to ruin you?" I asked.

There was a long silence.

"Bruno," Signore del Sarto said finally.

"Is he coming to your show tonight?"

Del Sarto sat up on the bed. "Of course."

"Good," I said.

"Good!" Signore del Sarto stared at me. "It's *good* that my greatest enemy will be there to gloat at my destruction?"

"But it won't be your destruction," I said.

"And how do you know this?"

I smiled in what I hoped was a mysterious way. "Because I have a plan!"

❂

quattordici

The problem with my plan is that it required that I leave the hotel, find Giancarlo Bruno, and give him a message. But I was grounded and Papa was working at the front desk—which meant I couldn't get in or out of the hotel without being seen.

So the next thing I knew, I was knocking on Brittany's door.

"How'd you like to go see Bruno today?" I asked.

"Bruno!" she said. "I hate him now! I just threw away every single one of my Bruno clothes."

"Are you serious?"

"I'm kidding," she said. She laughed. "I mean, I *thought* about it. But then I just couldn't. I hate him for what he's done to Mr. del Sarto. But I still love his clothes."

"So can you go and give him a message?"

"What message?" she asked.

I leaned forward and whispered it in her ear.

* * *

The rest of the day I sat around drumming my fingers and waiting for Papa to make up his mind about whether I could go to the fashion show or not. I was pretty sure he was going to let me, but he wouldn't say.

"As far as I'm concerned, you're still grounded," he would say each time I asked him (which was about a million times!). "Now stop pestering me and go finish cleaning all the bathtubs on the third floor."

"*Si, Papa,*" I said, wearily.

Finally, at 5 o'clock when I came to the front desk, he said, "Before you say anything, go get your mother."

I came back with my heart beating fast and my palms sweating.

"So, Gia," Papa said. He had his most serious face on. "Have you cleaned all the rooms I told you to clean?"

"Yes, Papa."

"You folded the towels?"

"Yes, Papa."

"You vacuumed all the hallways?"

"Yes, Papa."

"What do you think, Antonia?" Papa asked.

"Should we make an exception to her punishment and let her out of the hotel for the evening?"

Mama stroked her face and looked thoughtful. Boy, can parents be a pain! They were just dragging it out. Finally Mama said, "For one evening, yes."

Papa pursed his lips and stared at the ceiling. "All right then. Just this once."

I felt like a bird who was flying away from the nest for the first time. Something inside me lifted into the air and floated free. "You mean it?"

Papa nodded.

"*Urrà!*" I jumped up and down and danced around.

"Gia, please!" Papa said. "Not around the guests! What are you *thinking*?"

Mama put her hand on my shoulder and gave me a soft shove. "You better go get ready," she said softly.

quindici

*I*t was just like I'd imagined. Maybe even better!
Signore del Sarto had given me and Brittany
special invitations that allowed us to sit in the
front row, right next to the runway where the
models walked. There were limousines and movie
stars and a red carpet and paparazzi taking
photographs. There were people speaking French,
English, Spanish, and even Russian. And everyone
was dressed in clothes right out of the pages of my
fashion magazines.

The fashion show was taking place at the
Palazzo Pitti, an old villa full of art that is now
a museum. Outside, the palace is just a big, ugly,
square stone box with Roman-style windows. But
inside, there's no mistaking that it's a palace.
There is marble and gold everywhere. The fashion
show itself took place in the Palatine Gallery, its
walls lined with famous pictures by painters such
as Titian, Botticelli, and Caravaggio.

Signore del Sarto came out from backstage,

greeted Contessa del Forza, then came over to me and Brittany. "Where's Bruno?" he whispered. "Have you seen him?"

I shook my head glumly.

Signore del Sarto looked at his watch. "Ten minutes," he said. "If he doesn't arrive in ten minutes, we'll have to start the show anyway."

Just then I heard a hubbub coming from the door. Signore del Sarto looked up to see what it was. "It's Bruno!" he said.

Knowing about their famous feud, everyone was craning their necks to see if there would be some kind of confrontation between the two men. Signore del Sarto, however, simply looked back down at me and said, "I've seated Bruno right next to you. Get those shoes from him!"

I nodded. My heart was racing. It was bizarre enough that I was going to be sitting right next to one of the most powerful men in the world of fashion. But the fact that I was actually going to have to *talk* to him? It didn't even seem real.

Bruno passed through the crowd, kissing beautiful women on the cheek, shaking men's hands, smiling and making little jokes.

My mouth was dry, my hands were trembling, and my legs felt weak.

Bruno settled into the chair next to me with a soft grunt. I had seen him in magazines a million times. In real life he looked shorter and his teeth had a slightly yellow tinge. He had a dark, close-cropped beard and his head was shaved bald. His chin was wide and square, like a boxer's.

"What an exquisite dress, my dear," he said to me.

I tried to say something, but I couldn't. I just sat there like an idiot, blinking at him.

He studied the dress. "I'm sorry," he said in English. "Perhaps you don't speak Italian. Who made the dress? I can't figure out whose dress it is."

"It's a del Sarto," I said in English, my voice sounding thin and babyish.

His eyebrows went up. "I should have known," he said. He reached out and fingered the loop of blue silk on the front. "Though I'm not sure about the bow, I must tell you."

Brittany leaned over and said, "Didn't you know? Bows are going to be unavoidable this year." She grinned and gave me a dig in the ribs.

"Are they?" Bruno seemed amused.

There was a moment of silence. Bruno's gaze started to move away from us. After all, we were just kids.

"Say something!" Brittany hissed in my ear. "You have to say something *now*."

"I *know*!" I whispered back. But I couldn't think of anything to say. I could feel the clock ticking. The show would start any minute. But I felt frozen.

Brittany leaned across my lap. "So, Mr. Bruno," she said loudly. "Did you bring us anything?"

Giancarlo Bruno turned back to us. "Excuse me?"

"The note," she said. "We sent you a note yesterday."

Bruno looked puzzled. Then it seemed like something dawned on him. He reached into his pocket and pulled out the note I had written the day before. I recognized my handwriting. He read it out loud: "Dear Signore Bruno. We know what you did. If you don't bring what you stole to the Francesco del Sarto show, we will report you to the police." He smiled thinly. "This is your work, young ladies?"

I swallowed. Once again, I couldn't speak. I just nodded.

Giancarlo Bruno laughed quietly. "And what is it that I am presumed to have stolen?"

"You know good and well what it was!" Brittany said.

Bruno looked at us with a bemused expression on his face, like we were just a couple of goofy kids. Like he didn't take us seriously at all. "I'm afraid I don't."

"You're a horrible man!" Brittany said. "You used to be my favorite designer. I even wore that nasty perfume of yours. But yesterday I threw away every single one of your designs."

Bruno ran his hand across his stubbly beard. "My goodness. You must have been talking to Francesco. What kind of stories has he been telling about me?"

"It's not what he said," I broke in. "It's what *you did*."

The designer was getting irritated now. "Whatever it is that you're going to report me to the police for, I think you'd better spell it out."

I looked at Brittany. Brittany swallowed. We had come to the point of no return.

"The shoes," I said. "You stole the shoes."

Giancarlo Bruno's face looked completely blank. "Shoes?" he said finally. "What shoes?"

"The *diamond* shoes!" Brittany said.

The designer blinked, then looked around curiously, a puzzled smile on his face. "Is this some kind of joke?" he asked mildly. "Did someone put you up to this?"

I couldn't quite put my finger on exactly what it was, but Bruno wasn't reacting the way I expected. I'd expected him either to be mad—or to just give us the shoes. But he just seemed puzzled.

I looked at Brittany again. "Uh-oh," she whispered.

I felt a wave of humiliation and despair sweep through me. It wasn't him. I just knew it.

"Tell me what's going on," Bruno demanded sharply.

I took a deep breath. "Signore del Sarto had a pair of shoes stolen from him. They were part of an ensemble he designed for Contessa del Forza."

Bruno made a face. "Oh, dear!" he said. "Poor Francesco is in trouble." Then his face hardened. "Francesco really thought I would stoop to something like that?"

"Well. . ." I said. "We sort of convinced him. It seemed like you were the only one who would want to ruin his show."

Bruno frowned. "Typical!" he said.

"What do you mean?"

"Francesco is the finest designer I've ever met," he said, "but he's an impossible human being. He never trusts anyone. And he never compromises. Never. So it's no wonder he never gets along with anyone."

"He said you hated him," I said. "He said you wanted to destroy him."

Bruno shook his head sadly. "Our disagreement was never personal. Not for me anyway. It was just business." He sighed. "Poor

Francesco. I suppose it was different for him. For him, everything is personal."

Was Bruno just trying to throw us off track? I didn't think so. Bruno seemed sincere. I may not be much good at cleaning bathtubs or making beds, but I know people. Bruno wasn't lying.

I saw Signore del Sarto peeping out from behind the curtain at the back of the stage. He gave me a searching look. I shook my head. Signore del Sarto's face went grim and pale. Then he disappeared.

Seconds later, music began pulsing out of the speakers overhead. On the far side of the room I saw several people drinking champagne and laughing. And suddenly it hit me. Champagne!

And in that second, I realized who had stolen the shoes. It hit me like a lightning bolt. Why hadn't I seen it before?

"Oh, my gosh," I said. "I have to go!"

"What?" Brittany said.

"I know where they are!"

Then I stood up and began to run up the aisle back toward the door.

sedici

When we had gone inside the Palazzo Pitti, the sky had been overcast and dark. No moon, no stars.

Now the clouds had burst and it was raining.

Our hotel is about 10 blocks from the Palazzo Pitti. I ran down the road and across the Ponte Vecchio. The cold rain, whipped by a hard wind, sliced my skin. Cars tore by, throwing muddy water onto my dress. But I kept running.

All around me were the beautiful old buildings of Florence: ancient facades, red tiled roofs, old ironwork, hand-carved stone—it all flashed by. But I didn't notice it. All I could think of was that I had made a terrible mistake.

Champagne. Champagne. That one word kept running through my mind. *Champagne.*

My lungs were burning and my high-heeled shoes made it nearly impossible to run. Finally I kicked them off into a gutter. I didn't have time to pick them up. The beautiful leather shoes were swept up in a gush of water and carried down a drain into the sewer. But I just kept running.

Finally, I reached the hotel.

I burst into the lobby. A couple of Swedish tourists stood there, talking with Papa.

"Where is she?" I shouted.

Papa was behind the front desk. He looked up from the computer screen at me. "Gia!" he said. "What's gotten into you? Keep your voice down."

"Where's Cristina?"

"She's in her room," he said.

I tore past him and ran down the hallway to our apartment and into our room. The room was empty. Cristina's bed was made. There was nowhere else to sit, so it was obvious she hadn't been here since she made her bed in the morning.

And then I knew.

I ran back to the kitchen, pulled the key off the hook, and unlocked the door to the wine cellar. After I'd unlocked it, I grabbed the flashlight and ran down the stairs, dodged past the racks of wine and cases of soft drinks, all the way to the back wall of the cellar.

There was the tiny hole.

The thought of going into it again made me sick. But I had to go. I had no choice. I got down on my knees and began to crawl. I could feel the rock and the dirt grinding into my beautiful outfit. This time, instead of darkness in front of me, I saw a distant, dim light.

My first time crawling through the passage seemed to take forever. But this time I knew exactly where I was going and it didn't take so long. In my hurry I could hear my dress tearing as the wet silk caught on the rocks I was squeezing around.

And then I came out the other side. Knowing what was coming, I grabbed the ledge on the far side and lowered myself into the chamber.

In the middle of the room stood my sister. She turned around and looked at me.

"Give me the shoes, Cristina," I said.

She didn't answer me. She just looked down at her feet with a blank expression on her face. "They fit me perfectly," she said.

And there they were. The diamonds on the pale blue shoes sparkled in the flickering light of the torches that ringed the room.

My sister kept staring at the shoes. She was wearing her usual drab clothes. But from her knees down, her legs looked slim and graceful. Like the legs of a princess.

"Why did you take them?" I asked.

"All my life, I wanted something for myself. Something that wasn't part of the hotel. Something that wasn't making beds and fixing coffee and picking up stuff other people had dropped on the ground."

I looked around the room at all of Michelangelo's beautiful people, laughing and joking, having a good time. But now I saw something different in their faces. A trace of sadness.

"I found this place when I was about your age," Cristina said. "No one seems to know that it's here. No one but me."

"I need the shoes," I said.

But Cristina didn't pay attention to me. "I come here all the time," she said. "It's beautiful, isn't it?"

"But . . . what about the hotel?" I asked. "I thought you loved the hotel."

Cristina shrugged sadly. "I do," she said. "I love it more than anything." She took a long slow breath. "It's just — it's not enough."

I held out my hand.

"How did you know?" she said.

"The champagne," I said. "I was at the fashion

show and I saw these people drinking champagne. And then I remembered —"

"I had forgotten to deliver the champagne that Signore del Sarto ordered," Cristina said. "So I went back and knocked. He didn't answer. But I knew he wanted the champagne. So I went in and put it next to the bed."

"Cristina —"

"Then I saw the shoes. I couldn't help myself. I just slipped into them. And they felt . . . perfect. *I* felt perfect." She paused and smiled sadly. "I didn't really mean to take them. I just walked around the room with them on. And then I walked out." She shrugged. "I meant to bring them back. But when I got back to my room, they were so beautiful, I just couldn't."

"But you hate fashion," I said.

Cristina looked at me for a while. Finally she said, "Do you know what it's like being around you? Everywhere we go: 'Gia's so beautiful! Look at Gia! Isn't she fabulous?'" Cristina sighed.

"I'm not like you. I don't need excitement and beauty all the time. I like the hotel. I don't mind putting on my boring brown uniform and cleaning rooms. But every now and then, I'd like somebody to look at me and think I'm pretty.

Is there something wrong with that?"

Wasn't that strange? All this time I'd been envying her because she was so perfect, because she always did everything right. And here she was envying me.

"I'm sorry," I said.

"Once the police came, I knew I was going to get in huge trouble if anybody found out it was me who took the shoes. I was afraid they'd search our room. So I brought them down here and hid them. And every now and then I come and put them on." She shrugged sadly.

I still had my hand out.

Cristina had tears rolling down her face now. She wasn't sobbing or anything. Just the two streams of tears. A single tear dripped off her nose onto the leather.

After a second, she reached down, took off the shoes, and handed them to me. "Here," she said.

"I'm not going to get back in time," I said.

"My Vespa is parked outside," she said. "I'll take you."

We rode back to the Palazzo Pitti on Cristina's pale blue Vespa scooter. The motor putted and coughed as we steered through the pouring rain. We were both totally soaked.

When we reached the palace, Cristina and I walked up to the front door, the shoes wrapped in a paper bag. Cristina held an umbrella over my head to protect the shoes. The rain poured down on her head. But she didn't complain, didn't try to cover herself at all.

I could see my own reflection in the glass of the door. I looked like a wet rat. My hair hung down around my skull. The makeup that Signora Bernardi had spent so much time putting on me had run down my cheeks. And the dress? The gorgeous dress? It looked like a filthy rag.

A large man in a black suit stood by the door with a walkie-talkie in his hand.

"You can't come in here," he said gruffly.

I held out my invitation. It was tattered and wet. But the signature — Francesco del Sarto — was still visible in large gold letters.

The man looked at the invitation for a long time. Finally he lifted his walkie-talkie and started speaking into it. The rain and wind were so loud that I couldn't make out what he was saying.

"Hurry up!" I shouted. "I have something for Signore del Sarto."

I was shivering. Loud dance music was pumping out the door — which meant the show

was still going on.

"Gotta wait on my boss," he said. "I can't let you in looking like that."

"How long till the show is over?" I said.

"It's about done," the man with the walkie-talkie said.

"I have to go *now*!" I shouted. "Please!"

"Hurry!" I said.

The man just looked away.

"Hurry!" I said.

The man ignored me.

"Please."

He just stared out into the rain, totally ignoring me.

"Hey!" It was Cristina. "My sister's talking to you!" she shouted.

The man looked at her coldly. Cristina kicked him in the shin! That gave me just enough time to squeeze in. "Go, Gia!" she shouted.

I dodged past the big doorman and ran down the passageway toward the grand exhibition hall where the show was being held.

In front of me, the crowd stretched out down to the runway, where tall, thin women were walking out into the room wearing Signore del Sarto's fabulous blue dresses. As I entered the room, one last woman disappeared behind the curtain.

And no more models came out. The music continued to play, but it seemed like the show was over. There was a soft murmur, as though people were confused by the break.

I scanned the room. In the front row I could make out the face of Contessa del Forza. She looked furious. Had Signore del Sarto presented her outfit without the shoes? Or had he just not shown it yet?

"Stop her!" somebody shouted behind me. "Grab the kid!"

I tore down the aisle toward the stage.

Everyone in the room turned and stared at me as I sprinted through the room.

At the other end, another large security guard tried to grab me. I skittered past him and jumped onto the runway.

"Go, Gia!" a voice yelled.

"Hi, Brittany!" I called. Then I ran down the runway, past the curtain, and into the backstage area.

The models all looked tired and defeated as they changed back into their street clothes. Francesco del Sarto looked like an old man, one step away from his grave. Everybody there obviously knew what was going on.

There was only one model still ready to go onto the runway. She was a tall, red-haired girl and she was wearing the beautiful pale blue gown. But her feet were bare.

Signore del Sarto gasped as I appeared. I yanked the shoes from the bag. His eyes widened, then he snatched them from my hand.

"Here!" he said to the model.

The model slid into the diamond shoes and walked toward the curtain, hips swaying.

"Wait!" del Sarto said to her. He grabbed a microphone and put it up to his mouth. As he spoke, his voice boomed out over the music. "And now, for my final ensemble, an exclusive del Sarto design for a most distinguished client." He set down the microphone and pushed the model toward the curtain. "Go!"

We waited for a long few seconds. The music stopped suddenly. There was total silence, nothing to be heard but the clicking of heels on the runway.

And then sudden, deafening applause.

"Bravo! Bravo! Bravo!" came the sound of the crowd.

"You did it!" Signore del Sarto said. He grabbed me and squeezed me to him. "You did it, Gia! You did it!"

I grinned and squeezed him back. "With a little help," I said.

"Come with me," he said. Then he grabbed my hand and led me onto the runway.

The stage lights were so bright that I couldn't see anything at all. I was surrounded by darkness. Darkness and thunderous applause.

The applause kept coming and coming as we walked out on the runway.

I could get used to this, I thought.

diciassette

So that was six months ago. Since then I've been doing a little modeling. At first it was scary and weird having people staring at you. But now I love it.

I still have to clean bathtubs at the hotel, of course. But I feel better about it because I know that every once in a while I'll be dressed in something beautiful, standing under the lights, smiling and having the time of my life.

Cristina seems all grown up suddenly. She had a big growth spurt over the summer, and now she's as tall as Mama. The shape of her face changed, too, and suddenly she became ridiculously gorgeous. But I don't think she really cares. All she cares about is the hotel. Papa is always saying, "When you become the manager, Cristina. . ." And I don't feel even a *little* jealous. It's what she wants. It's what everyone wants. Sometimes she even cleans all the bathtubs that I'm supposed to clean. She doesn't tell anybody. She just does it.

It's our little secret. Well, it's *one* of our secrets.

Because I never did tell anyone where I found the shoes. We all make mistakes, right? And Cristina never told on me that day I was supposed to stay in my room.

And the room with the Michelangelo painting in it? Turns out the painting was a fake. You won't believe who painted it: Nicola, the pale-eyed man with the white suit. His father owned the little grocery store that was attached to the back of our hotel. When he was a teenager, he had spent months sneaking down there at night and painting the ceiling. That was why he knew about the little passage that led into our hotel.

I talked to him the other day when he came into our restaurant to have a cup of espresso. I learned two important things during that chat. One was that he said he had really always wanted to be an artist.

"Well, you've certainly got the talent for it," I said. He nodded thoughtfully.

"Maybe I should give my paintbrushes another try someday soon," he said.

The other thing I learned was that Brittany and I didn't have to get so dirty on our trip through the tunnels. Nicola told me that there was a much larger — and cleaner! — passage through another secret door. He promised to show it to me soon. That was how he had gone back and forth and kept his white suit spotless!

And Francesco del Sarto? His collection sold out immediately. The only complaint that the critics from the fashion magazines had was that there were too many bows on his clothes. What was it he had said? *This year bows will be unavoidable.* I guess even geniuses are wrong sometimes. I've been searching the fashion magazines for six months and I haven't seen a single bow.

But that's fashion, right? One day you're in; the next, you're out.

Now that the mystery's solved, I can step back into my role as tour guide and give you a peek at Italia and la mia bella Firenze (my beautiful Florence). Of course it's a very unique point of view because these <u>are</u> pages from <u>my</u> journal...

What if... I'd been born somewhere else? Impossible! Italia (or Italy in English) is all about fashion. My home town hero is Count Giorgio. He staged the very first modern fashion show for an international audience right here in Florence in 1951. I know it's not very nice but sometimes we laugh at the tourists for wearing tennis shoes to walk around in. Most Italians only wear them to do sports.

Wow, I feel like I've really changed from this adventure. I did so many things I wouldn't have done before. Now I feel like I can succeed at anything. Like...

Fashion by gia

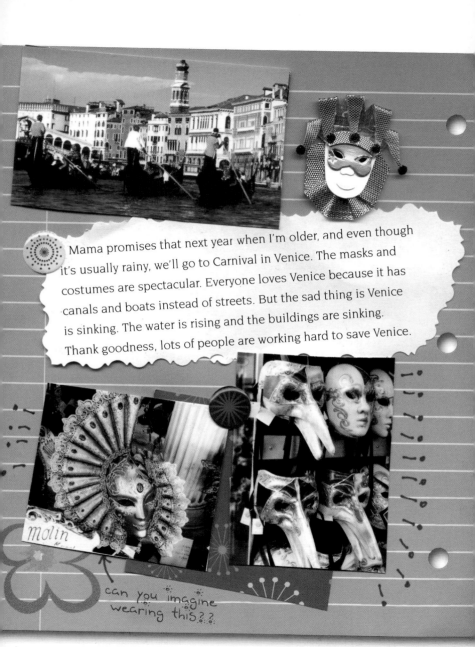

Mama promises that next year when I'm older, and even though it's usually rainy, we'll go to Carnival in Venice. The masks and costumes are spectacular. Everyone loves Venice because it has canals and boats instead of streets. But the sad thing is Venice is sinking. The water is rising and the buildings are sinking. Thank goodness, lots of people are working hard to save Venice.

molin

can you imagine wearing this??

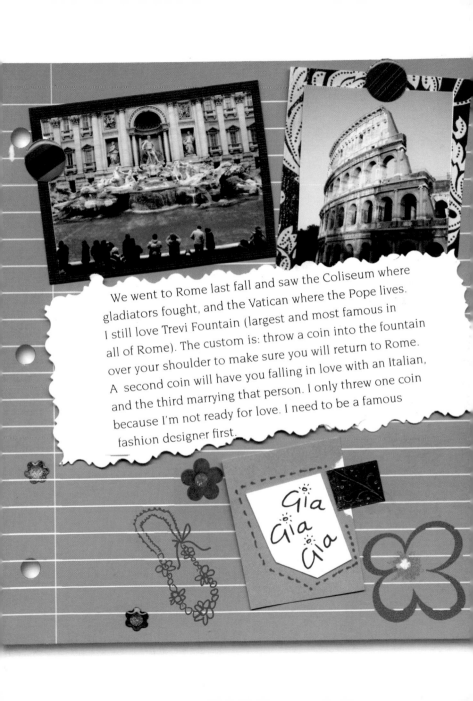

We went to Rome last fall and saw the Coliseum where gladiators fought, and the Vatican where the Pope lives. I still love Trevi Fountain (largest and most famous in all of Rome). The custom is: throw a coin into the fountain over your shoulder to make sure you will return to Rome. A second coin will have you falling in love with an Italian, and the third marrying that person. I only threw one coin because I'm not ready for love. I need to be a famous fashion designer first.

Gia
Gia
Gia

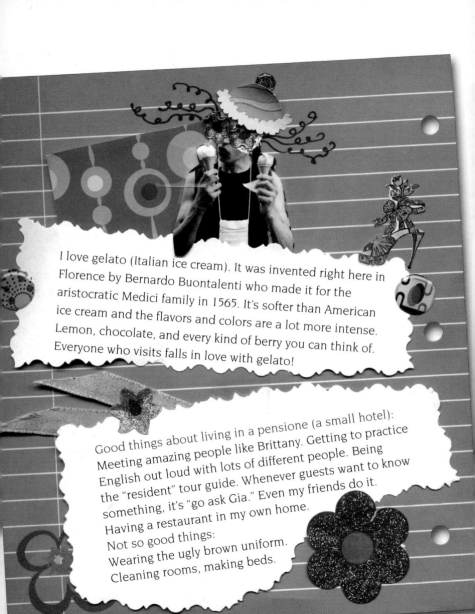

I love gelato (Italian ice cream). It was invented right here in Florence by Bernardo Buontalenti who made it for the aristocratic Medici family in 1565. It's softer than American ice cream and the flavors and colors are a lot more intense. Lemon, chocolate, and every kind of berry you can think of. Everyone who visits falls in love with gelato!

Good things about living in a pensione (a small hotel):
Meeting amazing people like Brittany. Getting to practice English out loud with lots of different people. Being the "resident" tour guide. Whenever guests want to know something, it's "go ask Gia." Even my friends do it.
Having a restaurant in my own home.
Not so good things:
Wearing the ugly brown uniform.
Cleaning rooms, making beds.

Fashion is an art and most of the best designers are well-trained artists. I never get tired of the paintings and sculptures that are everywhere you look. Michelangelo's David is at the Galleria dell'Accademia. David is the most recognizable statue in the world. I can't believe it, but once someone attacked it with a hammer and damaged the toes of the left foot! Ouch!!!!!

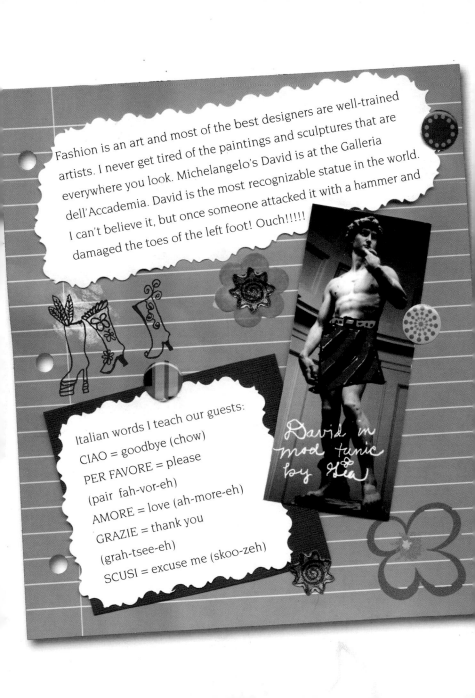

David in mod tunic by Lia

Italian words I teach our guests:
CIAO = goodbye (chow)
PER FAVORE = please
(pair fah-vor-eh)
AMORE = love (ah-more-eh)
GRAZIE = thank you
(grah-tsee-eh)
SCUSI = excuse me (skoo-zeh)

Art is everywhere. Just look at the Ponte Vecchio, the oldest arch bridge in all of Europe, filled with cool stores. I get to pass it everyday walking to school. Primary School is almost over (age 6-11) for me. But there's still Lower Secondary School, til I'm 14. Then 3 more years of Upper Secondary School. Now I go 6 days a week, from 8:30 to 1:30. I study French, mathematics, geography, Italian, English, science, music, computer studies and social studies. ART CLASS AFTER SCHOOL IS THE ABSOLUTE BEST.

Sooo pretty.
from one of the shops.

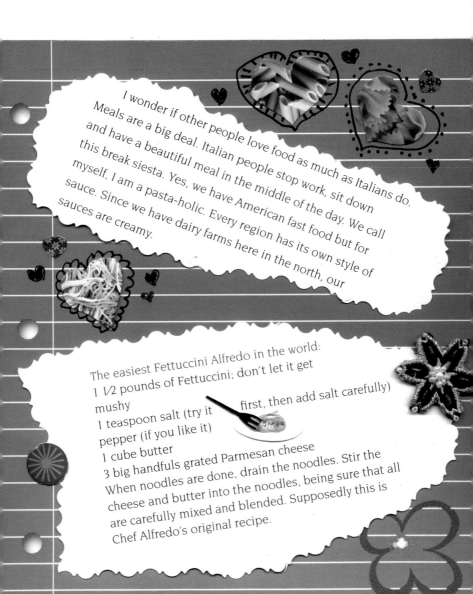

I wonder if other people love food as much as Italians do. Meals are a big deal. Italian people stop work, sit down and have a beautiful meal in the middle of the day. We call this break siesta. Yes, we have American fast food but for myself, I am a pasta-holic. Every region has its own style of sauce. Since we have dairy farms here in the north, our sauces are creamy.

The easiest Fettuccini Alfredo in the world:
1 1/2 pounds of Fettuccini; don't let it get mushy
1 teaspoon salt (try it first, then add salt carefully)
pepper (if you like it)
1 cube butter
3 big handfuls grated Parmesan cheese
When noodles are done, drain the noodles. Stir the cheese and butter into the noodles, being sure that all are carefully mixed and blended. Supposedly this is Chef Alfredo's original recipe.

Did I mention I love art? It's amazing to think about how the Medici family used their money to support artists and architects. They were such a big part of making the Italian Renaissance in the 1500's happen. I'll never forget modeling for the first time in the Pitti Palace. The Medici's lived there! Almost every year major designers show their clothing lines there. Art = Fashion. See?

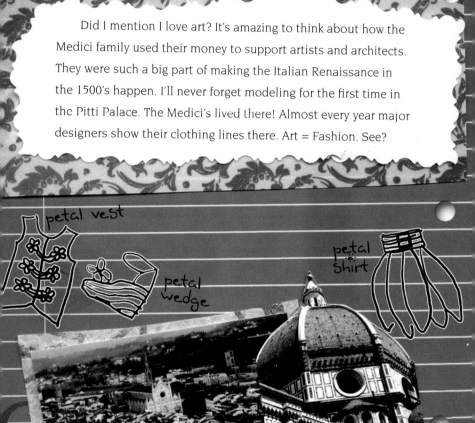

petal vest

petal wedge

petal Shirt

Firenze=Florence

remember Duomo??